Hack

Hack
First Edition May 2023
Edited By: Christine Morgan
Cover Illustration By: Christy Aldridge
(Grim Poppy Design)

Hack

By Stephen Cooper

Splatploitation Press

www.splatploitation.com
https://www.youtube.com/@Splatploitation
https://splatploitation.substack.com

Last Meal

Maybe it was the anticipation of the night ahead, but Jess could've sworn her double cheeseburger was the best fucking burger she'd tasted in her entire twenty-two years on the planet. It's not like she hadn't had The Burger Shanty's double cheeseburger fifteen-thousand times - or something like that - before, either. It was always a good burger, but far from the tastiest burger to ever grace her lips. It probably wasn't even the best burger in town.

But, tonight? Tonight it was fucking divine. So were the chips, or as divine as fast food chips could be. Could it be the anticipation? Maybe she'd look into that. *Google, does anticipation make food taste better?*

Sitting around The Burger Shanty's bright red table with Jess was her boyfriend Danny, who styled himself after the famous greaser, and Danny's brother Vince. Vince was the youngest of the group at nineteen, a bargain basement version of his brother. He clearly idolised his older sibling enough to try and duplicate everything he did, but lacked the natural grace and charisma of Danny, and his fashion sense always fell short despite trying to be a carbon copy. If Danny was a greaser, Vince was trash cosplaying as a greaser.

Lastly was Shane, Danny's best mate and the obligatory fat friend of the group. Shane was the pity party that Danny adopted to make cooler and be his muscle back in their school days. Danny hadn't ditched Shane after graduation though; he'd grown used to the big oaf, and if he wasn't hanging with Jess or little bro, then he was getting in to all kinds of trouble with Shane.

Jess took another hungry bite of her euphoric double cheeseburger, letting The Burger Shanty secret sauce dribble from her mouth. *Jesus fucking Christ, when did these burgers get so good*? She wanted a second, but couldn't fill up, not tonight. She needed to be at her best this evening. This was her moment to shine. She eyed Shane stuffing a second burger in his mouth with envy, but he lacked her focus and ambition. Also, he was drinking way too much Coke; *that better not be a problem later.* Danny wiped the sauce from her mouth with his fingers before sucking them dry and smiling lovingly at Jess.

"Hey! That was my sauce," she mocked complained, much to Danny's amusement as he kissed her.

Shane packed another handful of chips into his gullet, while Vince was eating less than usual. Normally, he fucking loved the place and went through a couple rounds of chicken wings, but tonight he hadn't made it past the first basket. He was nervous, and it was written across his face. Not the sort of nerves that made you back out of something, more the type that got you overly pumped before go time.

"You alright, little bro?" Danny asked, seeing the half-eaten wings that should have been demolished by now.

Vince nodded. "We can do this," he said to himself more than anyone else, like it was some kind of mantra. "We can do this," he repeated, ready to jump up and scream it at the top of his lunges. He managed to refrain himself.

Shane let out a loud elongated burp before apologising and then digging into a third burger. Luckily, Danny had bought way too much food, so there was plenty left for Shane to devour.

Danny had laughed the crazy amount of food off as being their last meal, although everyone hoped it wouldn't be. They knew he meant it in jest, a joke to calm the nerves - which failed on Vince - but the reality was, it could be.

Shane, being an enormous lad and not one to waste food, didn't care whether it was a joke or not; he was hungry. He started digging into Vince's wings as they remained barely touched. Jess couldn't resist any longer and grabbed a second burger too; *one more won't hurt.*

"You guys catch that new slasher flick last night, *The Handyman*?" Danny excitedly asked. "The one with the fucking *retard* who uses the garden shears?" he added, putting a nasty emphasis on the word 'retard,' and saying it a little too loud. He got a few looks from the other patrons, but no one was going to say anything, not with him being the chief inspector's kid, or with the enormous looking brute Shane sitting across from him.

"That bit where he stuck the shears down the guy's throat and opened them," Shane laughed, sending bits of chewed burger and chicken wings spitting across the table.

"Open wide!" Danny and Shane laughed together, quoting the movie and slapping their hands down on the table like it was the funniest shit they'd ever heard.

"I was rehearsing," Jess said. She'd wanted to catch the film, but she was a professional. Tonight had to go to plan, so, sacrificing a dumb horror movie was just one of those things. She'd catch it another night, hopefully with Danny. He never minded watching the same thing again; stuff like that didn't bother him. If he enjoyed it, he consumed it.

"You think the shear gag would work?" Vince asked, coming out of his near trance for a moment and nibbling at a few more wings while his attention was briefly back on them.

"I don't see why not," Danny pondered, as if trying to work out the physics of it in his head.

Shane nodded in agreement but didn't open his mouth again, as he'd moved onto a fourth burger and filled his cakehole with coke.

"Maybe you can find out tonight?" Jess offered jokingly. Only... he could.

They all knew what was coming. They'd talked endlessly about it for the last month or two, but now today was the day the subject had become forbidden fruit. They'd all gone about their day as per normal, barely acknowledging what was to come. Jess had made a few comments about rehearsing during the last day or so, but this was the first time the prospect of the violence had been directly brought up.

The reality of what they were about to do hit the table. They really could find out tonight if it was possible to shove a pair of garden shears down someone's throat and open them up to cut through a person inside out.

And that's fucking wild!

They could try whatever sick shit they wanted. Whatever twisted fantasies they had.

At least, that's what Jess had told them when she first suggested the idea. She'd gone over her plan, and suggested to the boys that, whatever liberties they wanted to take, go for it. The sicker the better. "Be as fucking depraved as you like, as long as I get to do my thing." she'd said.

That had gotten their attention, especially during the moment where it went from fantasy to reality and they realised she fucking meant it. That this wasn't hypothetical.

Vince leaned forward. "Should I try it?" he asked seriously, using his inside voice. "I mean, I really want to know if it would work." His ear to ear grin suggested he really *did* need to know.

"Wouldn't they think you're a copycat?" Jess replied, with a degree of 'I wouldn't do it' etched on her face. The idea of stealing someone else's material didn't appeal to her, not when they had free rein to do anything they pleased. *Why do something that's already been done?* She wasn't sure how the evening would go, but if the headlines in the morning read about a movie copycat killer, she'd be pissed.

If the focus was more on that, or violence in movies, rather than the violence they'd caused for their own fucking amusement, she wouldn't be happy. She saw too much of that already, and fucking hated it. Some sick fuck would do some nasty, despicable, heinous, savage act, and the media would credit a shitty movie or boring video game for it, instead of the artistry of the nut job who committed the crime. Fuck that shit. Sure, there were copycats and what not out there, but most fucking psychos did it for their own entertainment, with their own creative ideas, and deserved to be acknowledged for it. Why did the world always insist on blaming it on something that already existed? Why couldn't they accept and credit the ingenuity of the fucking sick assholes who came up with it?

"See how you feel," Danny diplomatically offered, clearly sensing Jess's reluctance. She knew he could stop Vince if he wanted; the kid followed him around like a puppy. But Danny also didn't like to disappoint his little brother. He was a people pleaser, as long as it was his people.

Vince mulled it over, like he really did want to know whether the shear attack would work, and when was he ever going to get another chance to find out? Maybe if they caused enough damage and the shears were just a single part of it, it wouldn't be considered 'copycat.' Also, did he give a shit? Jess did, but did Vince care if someone reported they'd copied the *Handyman*? Fuck, he might even be thinking he could make his new favourite horror flick some extra bucks.

Shane finished another extra large coke, his fourth.

"You're going to end up spending half the night in the bathroom," Danny joked.

"You better fucking not," Jess sharply added, and meant it.

That would just be awkward. You couldn't break into someone's home and spend the evening clogging up their toilet. She could already picture Shane's dumb face apologising to the family as he rushed to the shitter once again. *That is not how tonight is meant to go.*

*

Shane waved off Jess's warning. He always ate and drank a lot; this was nothing for him. Although, normally it was back at the apartment they all shared, not on an evening out.

If that's the right description.

Plus, he needed the food. He was nervous as hell. He may not have been showing it the way Vince was, but that didn't make it any less true. His nerves were pre-game nerves as well, rather than Vince's anxious energy.

And, when Shane was nervous, he ate. That's probably how he ended up so fucking fat in the first place. His dad made him nervous, he ate. His dad ridiculed his weight, so he ate.

It wasn't like he was *fat*-fat though, he always reasoned. Yeah, he was overweight, but he was a tall guy too, so it just made him a fucking unit. He was never going to be skinny with the way he was built.

And he fucking loved food, especially from The Burger Shanty. If they brought him here and didn't expect him to eat the menu, then they didn't know him as well as he thought.

Shane chuckled to himself. They knew he'd stuff his face before the job.

Danny's smile in his direction confirmed it.

Even Jess eased up. "If you crap yourself on their kitchen floor…" She barely got the words out before the whole table was in hysterics, remembering a previous incident at a friend's house.

The whole party had come to a standstill when, after thirty beers and a curry beforehand, Shane hunkered down in the kitchen and started unbuckling his trousers. Before anyone could ask him what the fuck he was doing, the first spray blew out of his asshole, causing a mass exit in more ways than one. A few of the less tolerable party goers added puke to the mixture as the vile smell hit.

Good times, not that the hosting friend thought so. When he'd tried to punch Shane for the disgusting act, Danny knocked him out, sending him spiralling onto the shit and puke drenched tiles.

That's how the four of them rolled; they had each others' backs, even if they were the ones in the wrong.

Though he *had* had to walk home that night, as no fucking way was Danny letting him in his Firebird un-wiped, trousers back up or not.

*

"Van ready?" Jess asked, changing the subject as the laughter simmered down.

"Good to go." Shane answered, still eating.

"Equipment packed?" she questioned.

Vince nodded his head and began tapping his foot. His nerves must've been really kicking in. He checked his watch, though there was still another hour to go.

"You go get the van," she told Shane, "and you do a final check on all of the equipment," she commanded Vince.

As they got up, Shane took one last bite on the remaining burger before gesturing that he needed to go to the toilet first.

Jess rolled her eyes, but only Danny caught it. Yeah, she'd broken the awkwardness with her joke earlier, but she was still worried. They needed Shane to be the fucking wrecking-ball he could be, not some child running off every five minutes to go potty.

"He'll be fine," Danny reassured her in his cool, laid-back manner.

She tried to offer a smile back saying 'ok,' but her own nerves were kicking in now.

We're really going to do this.

They really were going to break into someone's home, and scare the fuck out of them. Beat them senseless -- scratch that. *Destroy* those motherfuckers. Hopefully kill one of them.

Jess could feel herself getting horny just thinking about it. Her undies were soaked as she visualised the carnage and chaos they were about to cause. She was practically purring. This was *her* night. She'd been waiting for this from the moment inspiration struck. *Even longer in fact.* Tonight was going to be fucking wild.

She tried taking a few deep breaths, but it wasn't calming enough.

"What's my pre-job?" Danny asked, with a knowing grin on his face suggesting a solution to any butterflies fluttering in Jess's stomach.

"You can take me out back and fuck me hard against the wall," she said, then grabbed his head and stuffed her tongue deep down his throat while feeling his stiff cock through his jeans. He was already hard for her. She could always rely on Danny being ready to fuck on command.

"Yes ma'am." Danny didn't need to be asked twice. He took Jess's hand and led her from the table to the dirty alley running alongside the takeaway outside.

The final meal was complete and plans were in motion. This was going to happen. But first, Jess needed to be satisfied.

The Clarkes

It had been a typical evening in the Clarke's house since the kids returned home from school.

Todd, by far the quietest member of the house despite being the youngest, was in his room creating his latest LEGO Kaiju. He'd made three of the giants so far that all stood half his height. Not that he was the tallest kid; at ten years old he still looked about seven and was the smallest in his class, but for LEGO creations, half a small ten year old was still tall and impressive. He worked hard on them and added all the details the multi-coloured bricks would allow. None of them were replicas of *Godzilla* and pals, however; more his own interpretations. He loved all the old Japanese movies his dad had shown him, but he was a creative kid with a wild imagination, so simply recreating someone else's work wouldn't suffice. These were Todd Clarke originals, and he was very proud of each and every one of them.

He brushed his floppy hair out of his eyes, which reminded him once again of the dreaded upcoming haircut his mum insisted on him having. "Shouldn't be hiding your handsome face," she'd say, which embarrassed Todd no end.

With the digital camera he'd gotten for his last birthday -- nothing fancy, but perfect for the job -- Todd took several shots of the near completed LEGO monster from various different angles and focal lengths. He kept a running progress of the constructions for a blog his dad had helped him set up, which he updated every week. *Todd's Kaijus,* the page was called. It featured a host of LEGO tips, and designs for his original creatures. Once he'd made a few more, he wanted to start creating stop-motion movies, and maybe even start his own YouTube channel, although he was a little young for that at the moment. Still, he could practice. Todd returned the camera to its bag, satisfied with what he'd taken, and continued the construction of his latest creation, *MegaForceZilla*.

*

Todd's sister Elle was in her room despite it being her turn to do the washing up. She had been all set to help her mother out when disaster struck, as she received a message from a friend informing her that her on-again-off-again girlfriend Megan had been spotted with a cheerleader.

What fresh hell is this? Elle couldn't believe the accompanying photo of them holding hands near the arcades.

It was too much for her, but she wasn't the fire and brimstone type. There would be no marching down there and pulling the skanky girlfriend-snatcher to the floor by her hair and slapping her silly to win back 'her girl.' Instead, she burst into tears and sobbed into her pillow.

At sixteen, the photo was the single biggest crushing moment of her life. Some might say she'd had it easy up until that point, but that wasn't how she felt. *This is the end of my world.*

Her pale face began to redden due to the tears and she brushed her short blonde hair from her face, not wanting the loose strands to stick to her. Her cheeks puffed at the lack of breaths she inhaled while crying against the soft pillow. She tilted to the side, allowing her body to gulp up some much needed air, but that wasn't the sole reason for the lean.

Her fingers mashed the letters on her phone, sending Megan a message, subtly asking what she was up to, like she had no clue Megan was out gallivanting (a word her dad used that she loved) with Sophie, the ridiculously stunning cheerleader. Elle couldn't exactly blame Megan; she'd love to hold Sophie's hand too, but she found the gorgeous girl far too intimidating. Sophie was perfect. Pretty face, athletic body, bubbly personality, smart, liked by everyone... and gay? Elle hadn't known that part, not that she would've done anything about it.

Unlike Megan.

Elle wasn't a prude and liked to believe she wasn't as innocent as her parents believed, but compared to most in her school, she was. She just liked the more sweet, softer things in life. She was unashamed of all the *Hello Kitty* stuff spread around her room. Or how much she liked snuggling and holding hands and kissing. Sure, given the chance, she'd bury her face in Sophie's ridiculously perky tits, but she'd much rather stroll hand-in-hand along the beach ... like she did with Megan.

God, she wanted Megan! But it wasn't looking good. *Why hasn't she messaged back already?!*

Elle knew she didn't have an edge. That was something people loved about her, but also something used against her, and probably the reason Megan was fooling around.

She sent another message, maybe not the wisest choice so soon after the first, but it had been a whole minute and Megan hadn't replied yet.

Someone needs to take my phone away. It wouldn't be long before a third and fourth message were fired off too, with a mixture of whiny accusations accompanying begging and pleading.

Elle collapsed back into her pillow, disgusted by how weak and pathetic she was. She wanted to rip her room apart ridding herself of her childish ways, but cried instead.

*

Bev was once again stuck with the washing up, despite it supposedly being her night off from the chore. Elle had run upstairs in tears over her latest drama, and Bev knew there was no point coaxing her back down. She had a very emotional daughter who took after her.

Bev remembered those days all too well. The ups and downs of teenage love, *of which I had far too many*, she smiled to herself. A wild-child turned loving and responsible parent. A cliche, but not the worst one to be. She had a beautiful, sensitive daughter and a creative, handsome young son. Not bad for someone who once spent a night in jail for a pop-and-squat on a police car. Not her finest moment, but maybe her funnest one. She laughed at the memory. *If Elle knew half the things her mum got up to when I was her age ...*

She didn't really mind doing the washing up. It was a bore for sure, but also calming. A moment to reflect. They were due to go away on holiday in a couple of weeks, and Bev's mind was largely fixed on that. The things they needed to pack, the double checking of the holiday details, what to do while they were in sunny Florida. They couldn't spend *every* day at Disney, could they? The cost for one thing, but the walking too. They'd have to balance the theme parks out with sensible day trips and lounging around at the villa no matter what her husband and the kids thought.

She absentmindedly worked her way through several more plates while stuck in her organisational daydream.

*

Adam, having retreated to the downstairs toilet after dinner. missed the drama with his daughter.

He'd been renovating the small room for what felt like months now, but in reality had only been a week or two. Still, that was far too long. Bev suggested getting someone in to fix it up, but with the trip to Disney, that wasn't an expense they could afford. Not when he could do it himself, he had bragged, and now massively regretted.

What the fuck do I know about painting and decorating? YouTube made it all look simple; a five-minute job type deal. It had been anything but. He couldn't stop halfway and ask for help, though. The idea of some twenty-year-old kid shaking his head at his shoddy workmanship attempt was not something Adam could stomach.

He'd never considered himself a prideful man, but something about failing this simple task brought unreasonable shame to mind. He wasn't a fix the car, put up a shelf with ease, kind of guy, but surely anyone could paint a fucking wall and lay some simple tiles?

His brother Rob was due around any time, so at least he could get some help. Maybe even make some giant strides, if they didn't up end drinking all night and talking shit instead, *which is very likely.*

They didn't see as much of each other these days, both busy with family life. Rob had three kids himself, and lived an hour's drive away. They'd have to make the couch up for him if they did end up having a few drinks, but he wasn't above trying to drive himself home after a few cans, as he didn't like being away from his pride and joys for too long.

That was the only thing they ever argued over as adults, Rob's drunk driving. He'd never gotten into a lick of trouble with it and could drive just fine, but it wasn't a good example, and was still exceedingly dangerous in Adam's mind. As kids, they'd argued over just about everything there was to argue over, and fought just as often too. Adam always lost those fights. Rob was older and had always been bigger than him. But, as adults, all that bickering was long in the past, and they enjoyed the limited time they spent together. It was just the driving home after a few beers which caused arguments.

*

After several frustrating non-replies, Elle wiped away her tears and headed downstairs. She dropped her bright pink phone on the kitchen table and grabbed a tea-towel without saying a word. Standing alongside her mum, she began drying the various plates and dishes which had already been washed.

Mum put a loving arm around her shoulder and gave her a tight embrace. If Elle wasn't out of tears, she'd have cried. Instead, she continued to wipe the plates dry and stack them on the side, like she wasn't thinking non-stop about her phone beeping and Megan telling her it was all just a giant misunderstanding and they were good.

Elle knew that wasn't the case. Even without Sophie's involvement, they weren't 'all good.' They'd broken up and got back together more times than Elle could remember. Truth be told, they weren't a good fit, but Elle wasn't willing to accept that.

Her mum knew. She'd tried to talk to Elle about it after the last breakup, but Elle wouldn't listen. Just like Mum hadn't listened to *her* mum, and *her* mum hadn't listened to Bev's grandma, and so on. It was a daughter's prerogative not to listen to their mum's dating advice.

But she was right.

Megan wasn't a bad girl, Mum actually quite liked her. Dad did too. But they'd expressed concerns she wasn't the right girl for their sweet daughter. Too free-spirited. Maybe she'd be good for Elle in University, they said, but at the moment, Elle having not fully come out of her shell, maybe needed someone a little more, *'dependable.'* A quality Megan didn't possess.

Dad emerged from the downstairs toilet with his shoulder covered in paint. Somehow, he explained, he'd managed to tip the paint tin while it was stood above him on the ladder.

Why it was positioned there was anyone's guess. How he'd even managed to squeeze a ladder in the room to cause the chaos in the first place was also a question worth asking.

He held the side of his T-shirt upwards to stop more paint dripping from his shoulder and onto the kitchen floor, but it was only a makeshift solution, and he looked unsure what his next step should be.

"What am I meant to do about this?" he asked.

Mum did not help the situation by bursting out laughing, seeing him covered in paint and balancing a pool of it at his side. Even in her sullen mood, Elle couldn't help but break out a smile. *Only Dad could get himself into this mess.*

"Hon..." was all Mum could manage, before shaking her head. She grabbed the remaining cutlery from the sink, leaving just water in the basin. "Come here," she directed.

Dad carefully made his way to the sink, fighting his battle to keep the dripping paint pooled in his T-shirt rather than collapsing in a splattering mess across the kitchen floor. Mum helped him take his shirt off from the non-plastered in paint side and dunked the whole thing into the sink without any further disaster. Some of the paint had seeped through the shirt to cover his neck and upper body, but for the most part the exchange worked.

Now, instead of plates and dishes, the soapy water was sharing the bowl with paint and a ruined T-shirt. Dad stood topless in the kitchen, trying once again to figure out his next move.

"Maybe have a quick shower and throw another top on?" Mum suggested.

Elle could only laugh, a laugh caught halfway between how much of a klutz her dad was, and how embarrassing it was to have him standing there without a shirt.

15

"Made you smile," he said, pointing at Elle like he'd done it all on purpose to cheer her up. Then he left the room and headed upstairs.

Truth be told, she wouldn't have put it past him; he'd always found a way to cheer her up. His goal in life was to see her happy.

She and Mum both eyed the sink, watching the paint float and curdle. One look at each other, and they were laughing again, so much so that Elle didn't even glance at her phone.

White Van

The banged up rusty white van was parked on the quiet street under a lamp post that should have been lit but wasn't. Not for any nefarious reasons, just a stroke of luck for the occupants. The fact that the spot they wanted to park was under the only burnt out lamp just meant this was all meant to be. *Destiny,* one might say.

From the front seat, Jess and Danny spied on the house through the grimy windshield. The extra layers of dirt on the van weren't something designed to make it inconspicuous or hide its inhabitants *because that would have failed miserably;* it was just very neglected. Shane had bought it for pennies a while back and left it in a garage few knew about. Bought it for *this* job, with the expectation being they'd clean it up beforehand, which never happened. Life got in the way.

The important thing was, the rust-bucket reliably worked. and had enough room for the four of them and their gear.

The houses along the street were all a nice size. Not the wealthiest, but not remotely close to being poor. Every one of them hinted at enough money to live pleasantly, if not in gross excess. Each had a large front garden and a long drive-way big enough to fit two cars, along with big front windows overlooking pristine lawns.

Night had settled, so all the curtains were drawn, the sign Jess had been waiting for. The houses were evenly spread, meaning they could probably get away with a little screaming and shouting in theory, but not too much. The last thing she wanted was nosy neighbours or hero types ruining their fun, but she also didn't want to do the deed in the dead of night, because where's the thrill in that?

It was a cold night with a wintery chill firmly in the air so no one was out on the street. No dog walkers or runners. Judging by the amount of cars in every driveway, everyone was already home from work. *Another sign of the comfortable wealth some of us have never known.* When her mother had worked, it was from dusk to dawn; being home at a reasonable hour to cook her kid a meal wasn't on the menu. Those days had passed, however, and Jess had no time to feel sorry for herself. She was in control of her own life now.

*

Shane and Vince sat in the back. Vince tapped his foot, all his nervous energy building towards some kind of crescendo, while Shane had a pained worried look on his face. He may have occupied himself with trashy movies and takeaway food for the last couple of days, but there was no escaping the reality of what they were about to do now. This was life changing stuff. An experience few would live, and even fewer should have even contemplated in the first place.

After tonight, he would probably be a killer, or at bare minimum an accomplice. *All for Jess to get her kicks.*

It was far from his idea of a night out, but he couldn't be the only one not to partake. If Jess was doing it, it meant Danny was. If Danny was doing it, then sure as shit Vince would be tagging along. And if those three were involved in something, then Shane had to be involved as well. It was just the natural order of things.

He didn't have any other friends and none of the group treated him badly. Sure, they'd make the odd joke at his expense, mostly about his size or the dumb looks he got on his face, *especially Jess,* but Danny always had his back.

Danny had seen him through school and beyond. He'd transformed him from the outsider people stayed away from because he was a fucking weirdo to someone who was feared and even liked, albeit for entirely different reasons. Danny had set him up with a nice job at a garage, one he was doing well at and could possibly make friends within if he made the effort, but hadn't. He'd gotten Shane laid too… because that wasn't fucking happening of his own accord.

Maybe he'd stand a chance now, having been around Danny and Vince long enough to pick up a few things, but without their friendship, not a fucking hope in hell. He'd fought alongside Danny in countless bar-room brawls and they'd shared many wild nights together, getting into all kinds of crazy shit. No, if Danny, Vince, and Jess were doing this, then Shane *had* too.

Even if he did feel like he was going to throw up.

*

All four of them had changed from their casual wear at The Burger Shanty to plain black clothes. They'd contemplated masks, but Jess insisted they didn't need them.

They all knew what that really meant but none of them said it aloud. They didn't want to think about it too hard at this point.

Whatever happened in there, happened in there; no point worrying about it beforehand.

Loaded in the back of the van were a couple of unmarked duffel bags, a hard camera case, and a tripod. Everything they needed. They didn't bother with the typical crowbars and baseball bats for the break-in, although wouldn't be going in empty-handed.

What they most needed was the video equipment. It was all part of Jess's dream, her vision, which they all *had* to go along with, especially once Danny was sold.

Vince had stolen the video equipment from their old school.

While he didn't go there anymore, that didn't stop his ability to break into the place, something he'd also regularly done while attending.

Ironic really; he fucking hated the place during the day, but would often break in at night. Getting into the media department despite the equipment being under lock and key hadn't been an issue. Nothing beat brute force and not giving a shit. He was in and out long before the police arrived. What good were alarms if the response time didn't match them?

There had been some brief whining in the papers about the theft, but it was all soon forgotten about once the insurance company paid out. After that, the school didn't give a fuck They'd gotten their money back and then some, with upgraded equipment replacing the older stolen models. Vince was half tempted to go back for the newer stuff but Jess assured him what they had was absolutely fine. It wasn't worth the risk.

Vince knew he was never going to be a suspect anyway, what with his and Danny's dad being on the force. Despite their brutish appearance and wild nature, both their records were clean. If they were involved in anything, or got caught in the act, it was *always* the other person's fault. That was the universal truth, even if it was an out and out lie. Danny had once been involved in a hit and run, and it was deemed the victim's fault for carelessly staggering drunkenly into the road, despite Danny being over the legal limit himself.

Some people might think having a cop as a father would be a pain in the ass, but they'd found it had its advantages.

*

"Batteries all fully charged?" Danny asked, showing his own first flicker of nerves. He knew damn well they were; he was there when Vince checked everything. Vince indulged him with a nod anyway.

"How long will it take?" Shane asked, feeling like he had to say something after getting himself so wound up he might puke.

"As long as it takes," Jess answered, not taking her eyes off the yellow door across the street, and the lit window beside it.

There were a few other lit windows in the area, but overall it was eerily quiet. Like everyone had gone away for the weekend but left their cars in the drive. *Wouldn't that be another stroke of luck.*

Vince's foot tapping sped up once again like he was practising a drum tab. "We can do this," he uttered, like he did back at the fast food joint. "We can do this," he repeated, sounding even more buzzed.

"Thanks for the pep talk coach," Jess joked.

Danny glanced back at his little bro to quiet the fuck down. He got it; they were all nervous and eager to start, but they couldn't lose their heads. *Not yet.*

Jess checked her phone. Almost seven. As good a time as any for what they had planned, with the surrounding houses being quiet and curtains and blinds drawn. Hopefully the TVs undoubtably on in each household would drown out whatever initial noise they made.

If not, they'd have to face whatever came their way. Jess reached under her seat and pulled out a six pack. She handed a beer each to the boys. "A pre-match toast," she suggested, while cracking open a lukewarm one.

Each of them opened their beers and smiled towards each other. This was most definitely happening.

"To one hell of a wild night," Danny said, with an encouraging nod and infectious enthusiasm. He fully believed the words, and inspired that in the rest of them.

"We can do this," Vince echoed.

"To the *House at the Edge of the Park*," Shane roared, a little too loud, looking past Jess to the bright yellow door behind which their futures awaited. Grins from the other three let Shane know they got the reference and he hadn't just fucked up their 'pre-match' speech.

"To the experience of a lifetime," Jess concluded.

Danny leaned towards her, a passionate kiss turning into trying to suck each others' faces off. Vince and Shane bumped their drinks together and downed their beers.

The time was upon them.

*

Across the street, a porch light lit up as a burly man left the comfort of his car and walked down the garden path toward the yellow door.

Jess stopped the kiss. She'd kept one eye surveying the house, and spotted the new arrival.

"Shit," she muttered.

Danny reluctantly put the kiss on hold too as he followed her gaze.

"We still doing this?" Vince questioned, sizing up the newcomer.

He was a big dude, and an extra person they hadn't planned on being there. Not that they had much of a plan to begin with, which just made any deviation from it all the more dramatic.

"No fucking way are we backing out now," Jess responded, reaching for the door.

Shane started putting a woolly mask over his face.

"No masks," Danny reminded him.

"But…"

"You won't need one," Jess reaffirmed. *Oh it was so on.*

Vince pulled a wrench from under his seat while Danny slid on a pair of brass-knuckles. Jess grabbed a lead pipe while

Shane scooped up the duffel bags and pointed at Vince to remember the camera case and tripod.

They were out the van and heading towards the house before the mystery man had even rung the doorbell.

*

Rob Clarke neared his brother's house, feeling tired after the drive and having had to get the kids fed and ready for the evening before he'd set off.

He'd contemplated bringing the whole family along like his sister-in-law had suggested, but their youngest had been taken ill and it didn't seem fair bringing the other two and leaving him behind. *There'll be other times.*

He rang the doorbell while checking his phone for any missed calls, surprised to see there hadn't been any. Normally it felt like he and Nora phoned each other a hundred times a day, so an hour without a call was unusual. Maybe she figured he could do with a night slamming back beers with his brother? *Even if she does disapprove of his drunk driving, like Adam.* He had been busy of late, and really did welcome this mini-break, despite the drive.

He chuckled to himself at the thought of helping Adam with the downstairs bathroom being a break, but it was. Compared to running his own business and looking after three draining kids, spending a little DIY time with his baby brother was a vacation.

Plus, he couldn't wait to see the state of the downstairs toilet. He'd known Adam his entire life, and if there was one thing about his younger brother he was absolutely certain of, it was that he couldn't change a fucking lightbulb, let alone fix up a room. Look after and provide for his family, absolutely. Be a fantastic father and loving husband, pass with flying colours. Paint a wall, nope. Not happening. He snickered again as the door swung open.

"Long drive?" Adam asked warmly, sporting a fun *Elmo* T-Shirt.

"Not too bad…" Rob began to reply, before--

BAM!

Gate Crash

It was Danny's idea.

As they saw the two men talking at the front door, Danny gestured for Shane to put the bags down and charge. He'd carry the bags the rest of the way.

They even had a hand signal for the manoeuvre from back in their rugby days, or their drunken bar fight days. *It worked for both, despite being legal in none.*

Shane didn't think twice about it. All the nerves and apprehension momentarily evaporated as he looked ahead towards the targets and charged forward, unnoticed as they conversed, until, BAM!

Everything went spinning and flickered to black for all three men, to the soundtrack of Danny and Vince's hyena laughs.

Adam landed hard against the floor just inside the doorway, knocked off his feet by the combined weight of two massive grown men. A rib possibly cracked, the air most definitely driven from him. His head whacked viciously against the floor and he lost consciousness for a moment, unaware of all the noise going on around him. His back didn't need that kind of fall, either. It had been playing up of late and he pulled something during the landing. He thought he heard Bev scream, but that may have been in his head.

A couple of people stepped over him to enter the house. One brought his boot down hard on Adam's face, which caused another blackout as it propelled his head back against the floor. Lights out.

Shane ended up ass over tit, narrowly missing the door. He drove both men to the ground before rolling over the top of them and ending up on the wooden floor. He had a big dopey grin on his face, like he'd enjoyed some kind of gravity defying rollercoaster rather than assaulting two random men from behind, unprovoked.

For a split second, he wondered what came over him when he saw the state of the one laying unconscious beside him, *maybe a tinge of guilt*, but he instantly put that aside. They'd be doing a lot worse tonight. He heard the others enter the house and saw Danny drive his boot into the man's prone face. *Yep, they'd being doing much much worse.*

Rob had been the proverbial meat in the sandwich and got it worst of all. His head had collided with a set of thick shelves he himself helped install. He lay motionless, blood trickling from the side of his head and his neck bent at completely the wrong angle.

The shelves stood firm, *a fine example of his superior handiwork*, but also maybe the thing which killed him. Rob was long past caring. Nothing else had registered from the moment his head snapped gruesomely against them. If he wasn't dead, he'd probably wish he was, as he'd certainly never be the same again. His anticipated phone call from Nora went unanswered.

Jess could hear the wifey calling out, asking what happened and frantically making her way to the front door. One of the men's phones was ringing, but he was in no state to answer. Jess found and pocketed it anyway. *Can't be too careful!*

Last in, Vince closed the door behind them. Danny gave Shane a *'job well done'* wink. Then they entered the spacious modern living room, their eyes firmly locked on the wifey. She seemed dumbstruck at first, not registering what was happening with her husband and the other man just out of her view, but she backed away when she spotted the lead pipe in Jess's hand, and the sadistic smile accompanying it.

"Elle, run!" she called out, but Danny had already dropped the duffel bags and cornered the teen in the kitchen, cutting her off before she reached the back door.

Vince, as directed by Danny, darted up the stairs which led from the living room to the rooms above. Shane began to rise from the floor.

"Get out of my house!" the wifey screamed.

Jess laughed. It was a wicked, maniacal laugh she'd never used before, and she liked it. This was already feeling like the best idea of her life. She knew it would be.

The wifey opened her mouth to scream again and Jess instantly closed it with a whack of the lead pipe to the side of her head. She looked good for her age, Jess recognised, despite the insanity of what they were doing. Fun fashion sense, still trim and fit despite having a couple of rugrats and racking up the years in her forties. A pretty face that was undoubtedly a knockout in her teens and early twenties. *Star quality*, Jess mused. But now that face looked distraught and confused. New lines had appeared which hadn't been there moments earlier. Worry, stress, and anguish, accompanied the pain of being struck with the pipe. She lay mumbling on the floor with a lump on her head, barely conscious, looking like she had the weight of the world on her shoulders. And she wasn't fucking wrong.

The teen grabbed for her phone and tried dialling for help, but Danny was on her in a flash overpowering her and snatching the bright phone from her grasp. He showed her the brass-knuckles with a daring smile on his face. As the girl turned to run, Jess punched her. *That felt good.*

Colliding with the counter by the sink, the girl reached for a kitchen knife still dripping with soapy bubbles. Danny kicked her hand, the force of the boot breaking two of her delicate little fingers and making her squeal. It brought a bemused smile to his lips before he got back to business, pinning the girl to the counter.

Jess approached with a shit-eating grin spread across her face. The girl burst into tears, crying for her mum and dad to be ok, cradling her broken fingers.

She wouldn't have known what to do with that knife even if she had reached it, Jess and Danny both concluded.

"You need to shut the fuck up," Jess cruelly told her, pulling a roll of gaffer tape from her back pocket. She wrapped it 'round the girl's quivering lips before giving her an anything but playful slap across her cheek.

This close, Jess surmised she was probably right about the wife having been a stunner when she was younger. She could see that youthful beauty in the daughter, despite the tears doing their best to ruin the illusion.

Didn't matter, they'd destroy all the beauty before the night was out anyway.

Danny and Jess plonked mother and daughter onto kitchen chairs. They pulled several lengths of rope and zip-ties from the duffel bags and secured them. Neither of them were going anywhere.

Shane joined them in the kitchen, still looking groggy from the bulldozing of the two men.

"You woke up?" Danny laughed.

"Door locked?" Jess asked, more business than pleasure. She wanted to joke around and have fun too, but they needed to secure the family and house first.

Shane nodded and grabbed some rope himself before heading back to the entryway. He lifted Adam's dead weight from the ground and carried him into the living room. Danny brought a chair from the kitchen, as the sofa wasn't at all practical for tying the man of the house up.

"You good?" Danny asked, spotting Shane cranking his neck.

Shane nodded. With the adrenaline surging through his body the way it was, he didn't really have a clue whether he was ok or not, but he definitely felt alive. The nerves were still there, but he was getting into the spirit of things. He looked back towards the other motionless body on the floor. He hadn't checked for a pulse, but the man sure looked dead. He wasn't sure how he felt about that.

Danny gave him a playful nudge when he looked in that direction, suggesting it was an accomplishment rather than something unforgivable.

Like they'd said, 'an experience of a lifetime.'

Outside the house, the front door had remained unharmed during the initial attack and was now closed. The porch light faded with no-one standing nearby. The initial noise had made a few neighbours wonder what the fuck the racket was, but no one got as far as looking out their window to check.

It wouldn't have mattered. Everything else was inside the house and out of view. Bev's brief screams had gone unheard and Elle's phone was seized before she could try dialling for help.

The group had entered the house undiscovered by anyone other than the Clarke family.

*

Upstairs, Todd hid under his bed, *the safest place in the world to a young child.* He'd pulled his *Star Wars* duvet down to conceal himself, staring wide-eyed from his hiding spot as the bedroom door swung open.

He hadn't had time to get to the bathroom - which was the only room in the house that had a lock. Hiding was his best and only option. Todd watched as a pair of combat boots strutted into view. He despised other people being in his room. His mum and dad were allowed in, but Elle never entered, and he rarely brought friends around. He wasn't an unpopular kid; he had friends he hung out with, but it was mostly around their homes.

His room was more a LEGO workshop of sorts, not to be disturbed. It was his own private creative den, full of drawings and designs for future creations. Even the game console was downstairs rather than in his room, so if friends did come over they could play in the living room instead.

But now some strange man was in his room and there was fuck all Todd could do about it.

The man opened Todd's clothes cupboard door, making a big show of it. He crushed some loose LEGO bricks under his feet.

"I know you're in here, little boy." He spoke like he was the big bad wolf ready to blow the piggies' house down.

He went to a desk covered with monster designs, for clay work Todd was contemplating doing in-between future LEGO projects. After nodding approvingly at the designs -- *kid's got skills* -- his attention shifted to the three lined up Kaiju Lego monsters near Todd's window.

Without a second's hesitation, he booted the middle one, sending it crashing against the wall and into a dozen large chunks. Todd whimpered under his bed. He hadn't meant to let the whine out, but what the actual fuck! *Why would anyone destroy my LEGO?*

"You going to come out by yourself kid?" the man asked. Although it wasn't exactly a question, more of a demand.

When Todd didn't immediately emerge, he took a wrench to the remaining LEGO monsters, bashing the ever-living-shit out of them until nothing but collapsed bricks were left. Was like LEGO pulp. Any resemblance of what they once were was long gone. The new king of monsters had fallen. Then he ripped up the drawings too, just to be even more of a black-hearted cunt.

Todd remained under the bed, his hands tightly clasped around his mouth to prevent any further noises escaping with the hope that he still had a chance of being undiscovered, though he knew that ship had sailed.

A hand reached under the bed and made a grab for him. Todd tried backing further away, but the man's long reach meant he caught hold of Todd's shirt. Todd tried screaming as he was dragged out from under. The man placed his hand over Todd's mouth and was duly bit for his troubles. He let go, swearing, and Todd scrambled to his feet but he couldn't get around the intruder.

When the stranger cornered him and raised his wrench, Todd knew the game was up. He collapsed onto his bed, crying and wetting himself

"We got a bedwetter!" the man shouted for the whole house to hear. "Fucking pussy," he added, directed at Todd. He then ripped Todd's clothes from him, eyeing his little kid sized dick as he did. "Clean yourself up. I don't want you smelling of piss for the rest of the night," he snarled, with his eyes still looking someplace they shouldn't be.

Home Invasion

The bulky camera flickered on to the sight of Adam brutalised and tied to a chair in the Clarkes' expansive living room. He was facing away from his family in the kitchen and couldn't turn his head to them. The collision at the doorway had caused its fair share of damage, and Danny stepping on his face added to the cause, but he'd endured even more during the camera set-up.

While Danny and Jess had worked on getting the unwieldy old gadget ready, and making sure the mics were in working order, Vince and Shane had taken it in turns punching Adam. Blood dripped from his damaged head and oozed into his black, swollen eyes. His mouth missed several teeth under his busted upper lip, and his jaw ached like hell. It wasn't broken, and 'luckily' for him the same could be said about his nose, but both weren't far off. They'd only begun pulling their punches on Jess's orders after fucking up his mouth and laughing at his missing teeth. She needed Adam in a somewhat half decent state for his interview.

They'd saved the thickest rope for Adam and looped it around the chair several times. *He wasn't going anywhere.* Shane hooked some cables around him too and zip-tied his wrists behind his back. Secure and uncomfortable, just the way they wanted him. His T-shirt was soaked in blood, but it wasn't all his; some belonged to his older brother, who lay dead in the entryway.

Adam wept for his brother and pleaded through his torn up mouth for them to release his family. It fell on deaf ears. The night was only just getting started. The group carried on setting up, ignoring Adam's every plea, sniggering at his perceived weakness. Pussy. They stopped hitting him long enough to put up a couple of standing lights but that was as far as their mercy

32

extended, *and he should've been fucking grateful for the respite.*

They ripped the TV and console plugs from the wall for the lights and shoved back any furniture that was in their way to make room for their mock interview setup. Shane accidentally smashed a light stand into the 40inch TV, which caused the others to laugh. Danny was equally as brutal with the coffee table when it was in the way of the tripod, but that was no accident. They didn't believe in leaving things the way they found them. If it was in their way, they tossed it aside or destroyed it.

After wrecking the table, Danny decided handheld was the way to go anyway. A creative choice made far too late for the now ex-coffee table.

The camera was a bulky shoulder cam, the type used for broadcasting, as Jess wanted an *'authentic experience.'* They could have used the latest mirrorless 4K, or -- God forbid -- their fucking phones, but that didn't set the mood the way the heavy beta cam did. If it didn't have an XLR slot, then it wasn't the right camera for the job. The handheld mic ran from the camera to complete the retro broadcast look as Danny completed one final sound check. The gear was set up and ready.

Danny picked up the camera while Jess tightened her hair, making sure it was in a professional-looking bun. She reapplied her dark red lipstick and checked in her compact mirror for any more touchups. None required. The hostile takeover had gone without a hitch, or so much as a smear.

Jess stood alongside Adam in her reporter clothes, having changed from the plain black attire she wore during the break in to a classy plain green dress with a thick black belt. Looking nervous, she took a couple of deep breaths while Danny framed her. He kept the shot tight on Jess's face and shoulders, keeping Adam out of view for the initial image. He thought it would make a good reveal after Jess's introduction, along with then showing off Jess's gorgeous body in her figure-hugging dress. *It's all about presentation.*

"Do I look good, babe?" Jess asked as she got her nerves under control.

"You good great," he replied. "Sexy," he added, because she fucking did.

"Very professional," Vince chimed in as he handed her the microphone and put on the headset to check the sound under Danny's supervision.

Everything was set.

Shane moved away from the scene to stand guard in the kitchen for his role as on-set muscle.

Todd had joined his mum and sister and was also tied and gagged. He was dressed in his *Marvel* pyjamas, looking ashamed and scared. He hadn't been fully aware of what had transpired downstairs, having just heard his mum's screams, and had been fortunate enough not to glimpse his dead uncle. The sight of his brutalised father restarted the tears, which only exacerbated when he saw his bloody mum and sister tied to the chairs. He almost peed himself again but didn't want to incur any more of Vince's wrath.

Bev had fire in her eyes but could do little to act upon it. Blood had began to dry in her hair from the wound and lump created when Jess whacked her with the pipe. Given the opportunity, she'd wring that little slut's neck. She wasn't a violent woman by any means, but now the initial shock of the attack was wearing off, a thirst for vengeance and a need to protect her family was taking over, mamma bear style. Her husband had been beaten to within an inch of his life, and she still didn't know what happened to Rob -- but had to assume the worst, judging by him not being tied up with them.

She gazed around the kitchen at the mass of potential weapons, but all were out of reach. Shane chuckled at her like he knew exactly what she was thinking, and how useless those thoughts were.

Elle sat beside her mum, dejected and resigned to defeat, with her head hanging. Their phones had been collected and left within sight on the kitchen table like a fucking tease. Not that they'd be able to use them with their hands zip-tied behind their backs. Elle's broken fingers throbbed, and she wanted nothing more than to hold them tightly to her chest; instead, they hung loose, feeling ready to fall off.

Bev continued to watch the 'mock' interview being set up, still having no idea what the fuck was going on. Or why! She tried asking, but the gag muffled her words and Shane just hushed her anyway. That brought fresh tears from Elle, who was getting more distraught by the second. Bev wanted to rest a comforting hand on her daughter but couldn't. Once again, it was like the beast could read her mind: Shane settled his giant mitt on Elle's shoulder, causing the girl to squirm and the oaf to laugh. Bev wanted to cut his fucking balls off.

Jess nodded 'ready' to Danny as she clutched the microphone in her hand and took one final deep breath. Adam continued to murmur as he struggled to keep himself conscious. He was anything but fully alert to the goings on around him, and could well have been concussed, but knew he needed to try and stay awake in case he had a chance to do something. Anything.

Danny gestured to Jess with his fingers.

Three… Two…. One…. and action.

Jess put on her most professional formal reporter's voice and sounded like an absolute fucking star in Danny's opinion.

"Jess here, live, where a brutal and deadly home invasion has just taken place. Reports have confirmed one dead, and at least one more in critical condition."

In the kitchen, tears streamed from Bev's eyes upon hearing her brother-in-law was dead. She suspected, but hearing it aloud stung.

Elle's eyes reddened too. Her loving and caring uncle who had always doted on her was dead. She thought her heart was going to explode, but it couldn't. She couldn't let the same fate befall her dad. Her mum. Her baby brother, who looked littler than ever, tied to a chair in his pyjamas with his eyes tightly closed as if wishing himself anywhere but here.

Elle tried to hold back the waterfall of tears ready to spill from her eyes and instead focus on the rope keeping her bound to the chair. Whoever put the zip-tie on her skinny wrists had done a lousy job of it, and she knew she could slide her hands free, but she needed to loosen the ropes too; all made even more difficult by the broken fingers she was sporting. Once she'd loosened them, and escaped the zip-tie, she had no fucking clue what she'd do, but she had to try something. *First things first though.*

Danny zoomed the lens out, reframing the image on Jess and the brutalised father of the family. His head hung with his eyes glazed over. Jess continued her report without paying him any attention, continuing to look to the camera and Danny's beaming face. He was so proud of her.

"At around 7pm, the Clarke family stupidly opened their door to four attackers, leading to the death of one family member."

Jess bent to Adam's level.

"Mr. Clarke, do you care to comment on why you welcomed these fucking nut jobs into your beautiful home? Don't you care about your family? Why, Mr. Clarke? Why would you do such a thing?" she mocked.

It took everything they had for Danny and Vince not to laugh. *God she's so captivating and sunny in front of the camera,* Danny once again thought. He adjusted the shot slightly as Jess lowered Adam's gag.

"Please... leave... us... alone... please," he managed to cry through his busted mouth with the tears stinging his blackened eye. He was practically blabbering and it wasn't a good look.

"Cut!" Jess shouted, massively unimpressed with Adam's performance. She looked towards Danny, her brain whirling away clearly dreaming up ways of improving the scene. "Danny, can we have more blood? I really want the red to pop."

Danny handed the camera to Vince and pulled a knife from one of the duffel bags resting on the floor. Jess turned her attention to Adam.

"Mr. Clarke...Adam. I need more anger from you. This 'please leave us alone' bullshit just doesn't work, especially when you're sobbing like a fucking pussy." Her eyes flicked to his terrified family and morphed into a cruel smile as she saw Bev staring daggers at her. "I don't want sympathy. I want rage. I want hellfire! I want you to want to tear us a-fucking-part like your wife wants you too," She grinned knowingly at Bev. "Can you do that for me?" she finished, while holding Adam's chin in her hand and making sure he was paying close attention to each and every one of her words.

Danny drilled the knife deep inside Adam's thigh. Blood squirted upwards barely missing Jess's face as Adam roared, momentarily waking from his near stupor.

"Use it," Jess *helpfully* suggested as he fought the immense pain.

Bev cried and struggled harder, while Elle closed her eyes and did her best to look away and concentrate on trying to free herself. Todd's eyes were still tightly closed but he had no way of putting his hands over his ears and blocking out the sound, so heard his caring dad's awful wails.

Danny wiped a spot of blood that somehow impressively reached the camera, while Jess made sure her hair was still tight and her clothes were still straight before falling back into position ready to continue the report.

"And action," Danny directed over Adam's screams as the blood continued to gush from his leg.

"Police so far have turned up no evidence as to the motivation for the cruel attack, partly because they're not here yet, and mostly because they haven't got a fucking clue what's going on."

Danny moved the camera tighter on Jess's face. Ready for her close up.

"But speculation is rife."

Adam piped down as his consciousness began to once again fade. The roar turned to a desperate pleading unheard whimper while more blood spilt to the carpet beneath him and began to sink into the fabric, turning it a dark reddish black.

"Many believe it just to be a robbery, but so far nothing appears to have been taken."

Jess glanced sourly towards Vince, who held Adam's watch in his hand after liberating it during the mini interval. He put the watch on a side table with a cheeky grin spread across his grill.

"Other theories include a random act of violence. That the intruders just wanted to know how it felt to kill." Jess lingered on that suggestion for a moment, lust in her eyes as the thought ruminated in her head.

Danny zoomed in closer to her eyes capturing the menacing moment before pulling back out as she continued her report.

"Recent suggestions include gang warfare over territory," Jess went on, doing her damnedest to keep a straight face, ever the professional as the boys all covered their mouths with sniggers escaping. *"But this has since been debunked due to the man of the house wearing an Elmo T-shirt and one of the gang members being a ten year old boy in PJ's."* She turned and gave Todd a cheeky wink

that he didn't notice, as he kept his eyes firmly shut.

Danny pulled the camera back further, framing Jess alongside Adam once again.

"As the reporter on the scene, hopefully we can get the real answer from the victim himself. Mr. Clarke, what do you believe…" Jess stopped as she turned to Adam. His head had lolled forward while his eyes rolled back. She looked to Danny dropping the reporter character.

"Fuck! Is he dead?"

Bev's screams partly escaped the muffling of the gag. They were by no means loud, with a tea-towel taped firmly in place around her mouth, but if it wasn't there, the response would have been deafening.

Elle couldn't bear to acknowledge the psycho's words. She couldn't accept that her dad was dead. She worked harder on loosening the ropes, but it was a slow process, especially with Shane leering in her direction and stealing a glance at her chest every chance he, got forcing her to briefly stop the escape attempt.

"He better not be dead." Jess ranted, not giving Bev the attention she seemed to crave as her screams continued. This was *her* moment, not that old hag's.

Vince leaned in and checked Adam's pulse. "He's alive," he sneered, like he was disappointed in the outcome.

Jess took a deep breath and forced a smile back on her face. "Shit. That was scary," she joked. She held her hand out playfully, showing it visibly shaking. *All an act.* "Fucker nearly stole my moment."

She composed herself before turning back to the camera with Bev a blubbering mess in the background and Elle visibly blowing out a massive sigh of relief after realising she'd hadn't taken a breath since hearing her dad could possibly be dead. Danny nodded, indicating that once again they were ready.

"We appear to be having technical difficulties with our live feed to Mr. Clarke," she told in a somber voice before cheering up, *"So now it's time for the weather."*

Danny switched the camera off as Jess lowered the mic. He handed it to Vince before giving her a big warm hug full of love and pride. "You did amazing babe," he told her as he held her tightly in his arms.

"Yeah?" She asked with a smile.

"A natural."

Weather Report

Vince strutted to the kitchen to join Shane, while Danny followed with the camera. Adam stayed an unconscious bloody mess, unaware of their exit, as Jess left him on his own, following the others. She perched herself near Danny as he began to frame a shot of the rest of the Clarke family, while Vince and Shane stood between them, both with microphones in hand.

"You still want them gagged?" Danny asked Jess as Bev continued to struggle for her freedom.

The kids had both given up the fight, but Bev *had* to reach her dying husband. She *had* to save him. She *had* to do something! She was practically growling through the gag like a rabid dog, much to Jess's amusement.

"Probably best," Jess said, staring at Bev.

Bev didn't back down. She kept her eyes fiercely locked on the wannabe reporter with a look suggesting if she got hold of one of the knives, she wouldn't hesitate to stab the bitch to death. Jess liked that; she could use it ... *or have even more fun breaking it.*

Danny grinned at the family with his charming smile that Jess could never resist. "Sorry ladies," he told them in mock sincerity, "and little gent," as his gaze fell on Todd who still had his eyes tightly shut. The closed eyes wasn't a good look, ruined the whole composition. The artistry of it all. He pointed the nipper's disruptive behaviour out to Jess.

Jess sauntered over to Todd, smiling at Bev the whole way like an absolute bitch. Bev tried to warn her away from her little boy, but the gag prevented any real sense of threat. Just more muted noises, which Jess ignored. She knelt beside the youngster and gently rested her hand on his quavering knee. Todd tried closing his eyes even tighter as Jess demanded he open them. The little brat wouldn't comply. A change of tack was required as she released his knee and stood threateningly above him.

"How about you either open your beady eyes, or I cut your mum's fucking head off?" Jess suggested, partly in jest, and partly seriously considering it.

The young lad didn't want to risk it either way, so, slowly opened his eyes, staring at the psychotic girl looming in front of him. Todd hadn't quite reached the age of being into girls yet, but even he knew Jess was pretty. There was zero beauty in her from his position, though. He wasn't going to be someone who fell for the so-called 'bad-girls.' He hated Jess for what she'd already done to his dad, and couldn't hide the disgust and resentment from his face.

Jess spotted it, Danny too. Both gave a little chuckle; *how adorable.*

"If I see you close your eyes again, I'll bite one of your fingers off." Jess moved behind Todd and playfully snatched his hand, spreading his fingers out and wrapping her teeth around the little one.

Todd instinctively cried out and tried to pull his hand back as Bev kicked and screamed with the gag, rope, and zip-tie, making an absolute mockery of the gesture. Jess let the rascal's fingers stay attached, for the moment.

"You're so good with kids, babe," Danny announced as he looked through the camera at the much more pleasing image of the family all with their eyes open and in shot.

Adam made a whining sound behind them but quickly fell unconscious again. The noise was enough to at least let Bev know he was still alive, and she calmed down for the first time in a few minutes, despite Jess still giving her a shit-eating grin. Jess wasn't the one she had to worry about, though, as Vince hung over her with a mixture of nerves and evil intentions.

"How we meant to do this?" he asked.

"Just wing it," Jess flippantly said.

"But really sell it," Danny added, much to Jess's amusement; they burst out laughing at the private joke.

Vince and Shane refrained from laughing, not knowing what was so funny, while the Clarkes weren't finding anything fucking amusing at the moment.

Jess sat on her haunches and watched the action begin to unfold, as Danny called it. Shane stood awkwardly between Todd at the end, and Elle in the middle, while Vince moved from behind Bev to just in front of her as Danny adjusted the camera. Everything was set.

"I can do this," Vince quietly told himself, repeating it several more times, while everyone waited for him to start.

Even Bev was wondering what the fuck he was doing, and prayed it wasn't something extreme.

"Just have fun, guys," Danny said.

"And feel free to be fucking brutal," Jess added with a wink, still eyeballing Bev. *What a cunt.*

Bev began kicking and crying again but stopped as Vince leaned over with his mouth against her ear, his wandering hand grabbing a generous handful of her tit. "Don't you fucking ruin this for me," he told her with a vicious squeeze and a sharp tone in his loud whisper. He practically spat in her ear. He looked back to Danny, who again readjusted the shot like the perfectionist he was before calling action once more. Vince looked ready to begin, but then focused on his brother again.

"Are we going straight from Jess's segment?" he enquired. Danny nodded while Jess rolled her eyes at the fucking amateur.

Vince gave himself a few slaps of encouragement while Shane continued to stand over the kids like he was frozen on the spot, staring at camera in partial stage fright.

"Still rolling," Danny reminded the pair, shaking his head,

bemused at their thus far uninspiring performance. *Going to have some serious editing to do.*

Vince looked in the direction Jess had been having her interview with Adam, like he was carrying on the segment directly.

"Thanks Jess," he began, then faced the camera. *"Have we got some exciting weather for you today, ladies and gents!"*

Jess almost palmed her forehead, while Danny struggled with every fibre of his being to keep a straight face at Vince's hammy delivery. The Clarkes still weren't amused; apparently they no longer had a sense of humour.

Vince opened the freezer and rummaged around for a moment before emerging with a bag of ice-cubes. He grinned at the camera before tossing a couple at Bev's head. *"There's a cold front coming in from the ... "* he tried to work out what direction he was to her, *"east."* He peppered Bev with more ice cubes, several pelting her red cheeks as she unsuccessfully tried to dodge the humiliation.

Vince awkwardly passed the bag to Shane, whose face lit up with a big cheesy grin as he beaned a couple at Bev too. His were less playful than Vince's, smacking against the side of her head with force.

"And west," he chuckled, easing out of his stage fright.

Shane suddenly dumped the remainder of the bag over Elle's head and burst out in laughter at her shriek that couldn't escape the gag. Poor girl looked in a completely different kind of shock to the one she was already in.

"Unexpected snowstorm," Shane announced deadpan to the camera, with his big dumb face lit with pride at his clever joke.

That was it for Danny; he cracked up. He wanted to give his buddy a high-five but instead tried to recompose himself. He had a job to do. Vince moved from the freezer to the fridge and pulled out several bottles of water. He tossed one to Shane, who slid behind Todd.

"Heavy showers are also expected," Shane smirked to the camera. upending the water over the kid's head.

Todd shook off the soaking like a drowned mutt, albeit a tied up one. Shane's laughter grew, along with his smile. He was getting into this now. More confident. More daring. The stage fright had gone and was being replaced with pure showmanship.

Vince grabbed a bag of peas from the freezer and held them over Bev, who was still mortified at them humiliating her kids. *"We can expect to see plenty of hailstones as well,"* he directly told the camera, in the most unnaturally stilted way possible.

Jess may have had a flair for reporting, but Vince most certainly didn't. Jess couldn't see how he could be any more awkward in front of the camera. But, bless him, he seemed to be trying.

The peas hadn't left the bag despite Vince's reporting. He tried tearing a bigger hole in the plastic, but they were all frozen together. He squeezed the bag, hoping to pop them out like Smarties, but instead one big block of pebbly green ice fell through the bigger hole and crashed against Bev's skull, much to Jess's amusement. Shane almost doubled over in laughter, while Danny couldn't keep the camera still he was chuckling so hard.

"Her face," Jess screamed, pointing and laughing at Bev like it was the funniest shit she'd ever seen. It may well have been.

Bev tried turning to Vince with blood trickling from her re-busted head, but that just caused her chair to topple over. Another round of laughter exploded from the mean-spirited group. Shane dumped more water and ice over the kids, throwing it in the air like it was raining down on them. He didn't say anything; it was purely for his own amusement.

Bev, on the floor, tried to bite Vince's ankles, despite the gag still being in place, but he moved aside and punted her in the stomach. This caused even more pointing and laughing from Jess, as Bev puked and the whole 'scene' descended into utter chaos. Bev struggled for breath amongst the ongoing laughter, and may well have had a cracked rib.

The kids were screaming and shrieking from the water and the beating their mum was receiving, but it was practically a silent disco with the gags admirably doing their jobs. Elle was twisting and turning, trying to avoid Shane tipping more water over her, but the restraints restricted her movements so every drop was still hitting its target. *Although, on the flip side, they'd helped loosen the rope more.* Todd was shivering both from the water and the situation, his teeth chattering together and his jaw straining, all of which added to Shane's perverse amusement.

Vince spotted a pan of water on the stove after picking Bev's chair back up, blood continuing to flow from the top of her head and sick dribbling from her gag. A sadistic smile crossed his face as he grabbed the pan and looked towards the camera once more. *"But we are expecting it all to clear up and for there to be a heat wave,"* he announced, and dumped the pan of boiling water over Bev's head.

Only problem was, it wasn't a pan of boiling water. They'd had dinner already and the stove was off; it was just left over lukewarm water to soak the pot. It took Vince a moment to realise; he wasn't the sharpest tool in the shed.

"I was hoping it would be hot," he told the others in a 'duh' manner. *"Unreliable weather forecast,"* he said, back in his reporter role. He flicked the kettle on instead. More than one way to skin a cat ... *or scald a bitch.*

"All this water's made me need to pee," Shane announced, using it as an excuse for the excessive amount of coke he'd drunk at The Burger Shack.

"There's your warm weather front," Danny howled.

"Urgh," Jess said, but then it clicked what Danny meant. "That could work," she quickly corrected.

Shane stared at the pair of them. "What?"

A smug grin plastered on her face, Jess readied to humiliate the beleaguered mum even more. "Maybe another sudden downpour of..." she thought for a beat, "Acid rain," she suggested, with the sinister grin widening.

"Probably would be, coming out of Shane's cock," Danny joked.

Shane finally understood what they were getting at. "You want me to piss on her?"

Bev began wriggling even more, desperate for her freedom. Elle tried to cry out for them to stop but couldn't. Todd firmly closed his eyes again.

"What did I say?" Jess shouted to Todd, whose eyes immediately sprung open. Jess faked moving towards him with her teeth gnashing together as the youngster shrunk back in his chair. She stopped and laughed at the frightened young pup. "Last chance," she warned.

Vince and Shane switched places so Shane stood beside Bev while Vince rested a hand on Todd, making the kid's skin crawl as he gently caressed his shoulder. Shane grinned at Bev as he began to nervously unzip his jeans, not sure whether his friends were pulling his leg or not. He looked to Danny, who encouraged him to continue, then to Jess, who seemed fully onboard with the idea now.

Well, if no one minded...

"There's been rumours of acid rain in the area," Shane told the camera as he tugged his meaty cock out and let loose, spraying piss all over the fucking place.

It went everywhere. Over Bev's face and hair. Covered her clothes. Made a puddle on the kitchen floor. Even sprinkled Elle, much to everyone's amusement; the teenage girl looked like she wanted to hurl. Vince wisely took a step back, putting himself out of reach, and Todd was just about safe from the splash zone, although may have caught a bit of spray.

Shane just kept pissing. It was endless.

Jess howled with laughter as Shane continued to drown Bev with his rancid murky urine. *Why the fuck it's that colour is probably a question for another time.*

As the piss slowed, Shane grabbed Bev's head and turned her towards him. He quickly whipped off the tea towel gag and jammed his fat, now fully erect, dick in her mouth. Apparently pissing in front of a room full of people over a total stranger was quite the turn on.

Before Bev even knew what he'd done, or had a chance to bite down and sever his foul tool, his dick was back out of her mouth, having left a drizzle of piss in there. He slapped her across the face with his cock too, as his dumb grin grew wider. *What a time to be alive.* He replaced the gag on the stunned, piss-soaked, and mouth-raped, mum.

"And that concludes the weather," he told the camera as he smugly zipped back up, to Danny and Jess clapping with rapacious applauds

Before they could work out the next segment Elle's phone buzzed on the kitchen counter.

Scandal

Jess grabbed the bright pink phone from the kitchen table and read the partial message on display aloud.

"Why do I have 20 messages from you Elle. It's a bit weird…"

Elle's tears stopped. Embarrassment took over as the psychotic cunt plaguing her family further invaded her private life. Her cheeks reddened with each word read. Once again she wanted to bury her face in her pillow, but also wanted to know what the rest of Megan's message said. *Life can be a real bitch.*

"That it?" Shane asked, curious for more.

"You and your gossip," Danny laughed. "Like an old woman."

"What? I like to know what's going on." His wide grin suggested this could very well be his favourite part of the night, despite already killing a man, pissing over a family, and sticking his dick in a MILF's mouth.

"There's more, but…" Jess carefully avoided the pool of murky piss gathered on the floor between mother and daughter, courtesy of Shane's rampant dick, as she approached Elle.

She aimed the phone at the girl's face, allowing the facial recognition to do its thing. The phone sprang to life, revealing Elle's *Hello Kitty* wallpaper, which brought an instant eye-roll from Jess.

"*Hello Kitty?*" she asked, in the most condescending voice she could muster to support the mocking eye-roll. She flicked the rest of the message open and held her chest like she was reading lines from an am-dram.

"This is from Megan," she told the gang, who'd all briefly stopped their torment of the family.

Adam groaned behind them, momentarily regaining consciousness, but Danny told him to keep it the fuck down, not wanting the spotlight taken from his girl as she prepared her piece.

Jess began her reading. She put on a valley girl voice, deeming it appropriate for Megan. *Creative choice.*

"Why do I have like 20 new messages from you Elle. It's a bit weird. I thought I made it clear we're not together anymore. You're sweet and all, and I had a good time with you, and I'm sorry it ended the way it did, but you can't be stalking me like this. It's been weeks. You really need to stop messaging me."

"She a rug-muncher?" Vince asked smirking at Elle while giving Todd's shoulder another squeeze.

"I don't know," Jess replied, looking at Elle in mock seriousness. "You a dyke, Elle?" she asked in her cruelest voice, making a show of it for Bev, who was once again ready to fucking straight up cut the bitch.

All eyes were on Elle, but at least they'd stopped hurting her family. Elle nodded, bringing another mean smile from Jess.

"Let's do another segment." Jess happily squealed, clapping her hands together in excitement. She thought about what to call it before an eureka moment struck. "Current Affairs," she joked, bringing a laugh from the group, with the Clarkes again being boring fucks and not joining in the fun.

Jess knelt in front of Elle, again being careful to avoid the puddle of piss. "I'm going to take off your gag so we can have a girl chat," she said. "But if you try and scream, the gag is going back on, and your mum and brother are going to get fucked up."

Shane took position behind Bev with a crude smile and a lick of his lips. Vince remained too close to Todd.

"You understand?" Jess pressed.

Elle nodded, fresh tears in her formerly bright eyes from Megan's reply, along with Jess's threat. *This is all too much!* She wished she was back upstairs, crying into her pillow about

Megan. That would be better than being tied to a chair with broken fingers, her uncle dead and her dad beaten to within an inch of his life, while these assholes threatened what remained of her family. Suddenly the drama with Megan was preferable. Familiar.

Jess grabbed the corner of the gaffer tape and began to very slowly peel it from Elle's lips, making sure to cause maximum pain. Elle's sobs intensified, which only made Jess even less hurried. Elle took some much needed breaths from the corner of her mouth as the tape released its grasp, thankful for the small mercy, even though that wasn't Jess's intention. She just wanted to hurt the girl more, and was revelling in it.

Danny moved closer with the camera so just their two faces were in frame. He wanted to shoot the segment a little different, as it wasn't planned, and allowed him a little spontaneity and creativeness with the camerawork.

"Ready when you are babe," he told Jess as she finally finished peeling the gaffer tape from Elle's mouth. The girl was now gulping down air to the point of almost choking on it.

Jess straightened her hair and brushed her dress down once more. She cleared her throat a few times and took a deep breath herself as she went back into reporter mode.

Vince passed her the microphone while Adam continued to moan in the background, dipping in and out of reality with his distracting groans. Shane put the second mic down on the kitchen table, strutted over to Adam, and knocked him the fuck out with a nasty punch that caught him on the chin and instantly shut him the hell up. Jess nodded her approval, while Bev tried kicking her legs out and screaming, but again failed to achieve either. Shane retook his place next to her, giving her a wink like he'd just defended her honour rather than punch her helpless husband in the face.

"And ... action," Danny called, on Jess's sign that she was ready.

"Jess here in Current Affairs, and boy do we have an affair for you." She quickly skimmed several messages, getting caught up. *"Wow. So, Elle, you're a right little psycho, aren't you? You really did send her like twenty messages without reply? You're fucking cra-cra! What do you have to say for yourself young lady?"*

"What'd they say?" Shane interrupted, breaking the illusion of the segment as he sought after more scandalous details.

Bev continued to struggle for freedom that wouldn't come. Her eyes filled with rage and hatred. Physically harming her family was unforgivable, but trying to humiliate her daughter like this…

Jess tried to keep the segment going while also answering Shane's question. She really did consider herself a pro.

"So, Elle, your cool-looking ex apparently hooked up with a super hot cheerleader? Meanwhile, you couldn't accept that you weren't a couple anymore and begged your girl Megan back. Is that true?" She aimed the microphone at Elle.

"Nice," Shane said aloud at the juicy gossip, before clamping his hand over his mouth in an attempt not to ruin the piece.

"Please let us go," Elle managed to plead quietly with her head bowed, as Jess practically stuck the mic up her nose to hear her response.

"You're not going anywhere, bitch. Can forget that," Vince sternly told her, so Jess didn't have to break character.

"Why are you doing this?" Elle whined.

"I'll ask the questions," Jess sharply responded, breaking her bit for the moment she took the mic back. "One more question like that, and someone's getting hurt."

Elle tried to shake the tears from her eyes, but they remained stained to her face, along with some left over droplets of piss.

Jess changed tack, not giving up on the piece yet despite

Elle's less than stellar performance. *"Elle, the audience is dying to know. Why'd Megan break up with you?"* She aimed the mic back in Elle's face while she continued to scroll though the girl's phone.

Elle kept quiet, and hung her head even lower, if that was possible. Upset, hurt, and thoroughly embarrassed. If the pain in her broken fingers didn't kill her, shame would.

Vince applied more pressure to Todd's shoulder, squeezing it to the point the lad yelped through his gag, making sure that Elle got the message. *Answer the fucking question.*

"Please?" Elle softly tried again, to another shake of the head from Jess.

Elle looked to her mum for support not knowing what to do or say. Vince dug his claws into Todd, eliciting a muffled scream. He wasn't far off wetting himself again.

Bev looked her daughter in the eyes, desperate to help, but there was nothing she could do.

Elle faced Jess with no other option.

"She said I was lovely, but not right for her," Elle quietly replied, hoping only Jess would hear. Shane's obnoxious whistle and shake of the head suggested she failed.

"So, you're boring?" Jess instantly replied. Danny kept the camera locked on the two of them making sure to capture the hurt in Elle's eyes.

"I try not to be," Elle muttered, much to Jess's bemusement and bringing an arrogant smirk to Vince's face. He was a lot of things, but at least he wasn't boring.

"But you are. I mean, one look at your phone tells me that. Hello Kitty wallpaper. Fucking Candy Crush and Angry Birds? Your Google history reads like a fucking 19th century country girl. Places to go for long walks. Cookie recipes. Make-up tips. Boring as fuck."

Bev's eyes switched from pure hatred to pleading for them to please stop. Jess had no intention of stopping.

"Your gallery is full of fucking cat memes and unicorns and positive sayings with colourful backgrounds." She made a vomit sound, putting her fingers in her mouth and getting a round of laughter from the lads.

Danny zoomed into Elle, ready to capture the moment where Jess broke her. It was coming.

"Your notes app is like a fucking diary." Jess cleared her throat, once again ready to read the personal notes meant for no-one other than Elle.

"Feeling blue today. I cut my hair and Megan didn't even notice." Jess could barely keep a straight face. Scrolled further *"I kinda hate that Mum brought me this baby looking yellow top today and that I love it. What's wrong with me?"* Jess smiled to Bev, giving her an 'aww' in the process while the boys sniggered.

Bev tried giving her daughter a supportive smile but Elle's head was still down.

"Oh shit!" Jess said aloud, fully breaking her reporter 'character' and beaming with pride at her discovery. "Maybe I was wrong. We've got a nude selfie!"

She thrust the phone in front of Bev, making sure she got a good look at her daughter's naked body. Shane also got a good eyeful. Jess showed the picture to Todd with a little wink to suggest he should enjoy that, while Vince gawked at it too.

"Look at those itty-bitty-titties. I didn't think you had it in you to send something like this."

She showed Danny the picture for the camera while keeping her eyes on Elle who was beyond mortified.

"You thought, one look at that young tight body she'd come running back, right?" Jess laughed. "Wasn't expecting the big-titted smoking hot super fuckable cheerleader with the killer ass to swoop in?"

Elle didn't answer. She just cried at the fact that Jess was one-hundred-percent right while listening to the bitch's patronising laugh.

"What are you, like, twelve, with tits that tiny?" Jess asked.

Elle didn't reply until Shane slapped Bev across the face, leaving a red mark to go with the other still on display after his previous slap.

"Sixteen," Elle shouted, not wanting her mum to take any more abuse.

"Jesus. You get disability for those?" Jess mocked.

"Fuck you," Elle whispered, just audible enough for Jess to hear and bring a smile to her face.

"I don't go that way." She looked to Danny. "Got myself a real man." She grabbed his crotch through his jeans, much to his delight. The camera wobbled for a moment but he'd sort it in post.

"Maybe that's what *she* needs," Shane suggested.

Any pretence of a news segment had been dropped. Jess just wanted to ruin the girl.

"You think a big dick in you might help?" she asked Elle, whose worry increased ten-fold. "What do you reckon, Mum? Should we fix your girl?"

Jess nodded for Bev's gag to be lowered, while Vince pulled a bread knife from the kitchen counter and put it across Todd's throat. *No verbal warning required.*

"My daughter doesn't need fixing." Bev tried her best to sound proud and strong despite the abuse she'd endured and witnessed.

"Maybe she needs some *little* dick in her instead." Jess looked towards Todd, daring Bev to cause a scene.

Bev didn't take the bait, just shook her head.

Jess refocused on Elle. "What do you say, girl? You damn well know fingers don't count; want one of the lads here to take your V-Plates from you? Which one do you fancy?"

"I'm game." Shane said, a little too loud and excited. "Can start with a blowie just like your whore mum." He crudely laughed.

If that dick comes near my mouth again, I'll be biting it off, Bev thought in disgust

"You got a good look at Shane's fat cock right? That would fix you?" Jess was enjoying every second of destroying the teen girl, and it was written all over her face. The pure ecstasy of it all could have been a worry, if it wasn't exactly the reaction within herself she was hoping for. Jess knew she was a cunt, but was taking every bit of delight in discovering just how much of one she was.

"There's nothing wrong with me," Elle stated, with a hint of strength in her voice. She meant it, too, much to Jess's amusement.

Shane looked disappointed, but taking her without her consent was still a very real option, *and definitely more fun.*

"I'm just fucking with you," Jess told Elle, like she needed to lighten up. "Hell, I'd have a little nibble between your legs myself if I wasn't so busy brutalising your family and getting ready to kill your cowardly pathetic loser of a father."

Elle spat in Jess's face without warning.

No hacking it up, or thinking about it first, just a purely instinctive gob that landed in Jess's left eye and dribbled down her nose onto her chin.

"You cunt!" Jess screamed at the young bitch before giving her a vicious slap that knocked Elle backwards and caused the chair to tip.

The three guys cheered Jess on with a round of 'ohhhs.'

Jess kicked Elle in the gut, causing the teen to scream in pain before receiving another kick to her tits. Jess pulled her leg back again and punted Elle in the face, making a couple of teeth spill from her busted mouth and knocking her out, stopping the cries.

She spotted the bread knife in Vince's hand, "Pass me that," Jess demanded with a look of savagery in her eyes.

Vince handed her the knife while Bev kicked up a fuss, still not learning, or accepting, how little she could do.

"Gonna cut off what little God gave you," Jess told the unconscious Elle ripping at her shirt.

A loud groan interrupted the attack. The group spun towards Adam, but he was still completely out of it. The noise was coming from even further back.

"What the hell?" Jess mouthed, as they all looked in the direction of the front door.

The Dead Rise

Rob lay in the doorway of the Clarkes' house as close to death as you could get without holding hands with the Reaper himself. White as a ghost, which he practically was. His neck was at an angle necks shouldn't be at, and he couldn't move a single inch of his body. His left arm was contorted in a disgusting manner, but luckily he couldn't feel a thing. He'd managed to let out a whimpering moan as the realisation of his impending death struck him, but had been unaware of the brutality going on. He was concussed, not sound of mind, and a fucking potato. Rob's days were done, and why his body and mind hadn't completely given up on him yet was a mystery.

Danny was the first to reach the entryway and recognise the source of the noise. He knelt by the broken man, looking into his eyes for any sign of coherence. Rob's eyes were more pleading than angry. Danny wasn't sure if the pleading was for medical attention, or to be put down and for the suffering and indignity to end.

Vince, seeing Rob moaning, put his back against the front door to stop any escape attempt happening, but Rob wasn't going anywhere.

Shane arrived next, looking to Rob with morbid curiosity, unsure how he felt about the man being alive after thinking he'd killed him. He'd tried not to think about it after they'd got into the swing of things, but now the Ghost of Christmas Past was making some kind of wounded whiny sound like a run-over mutt, and all Shane wanted was for him to shut the fuck up. He stayed a little further back than Danny and Vince.

Jess was the last on the scene, and she'd brought the camera and mic, with her gaze hard against the eye piece and an excited grin on her face. Framing Danny in the shot with Vince's legs prominent behind him, she panned the camera, taking in the horrific state of Rob which grew her smile even more.

Danny instantly knew what to do as Jess gave him the mic.

"Danny here with Patient Zero as the zombie apocalypse begins," he announced in the cheesiest reporter impression he could muster, still seeming way cooler than either Vince or Shane's attempts.

He mocked worry and terror, really hamming it up for the camera like he was in a 50s sci-fi B-movie filled with killer crabs or giant ants before his expression slipped into amusement. Very unprofessional, but he shook off his smirk and got back to business.

"Just moments ago, this man was a confirmed kill in a brutal home invasion. Dead. Gone. Done. Not coming back…" He moved close to the camera, with his playful face taking up the entire frame. *"But now … he's back,"* he told the potential audience in a 'coming to get you Barbara,' tone.

Chuckling, Jess pushed Danny back into focus with the cheesy grin still plastered across his smug face. He was having a whale of a time.

He continued his report, including Rob in the conversation. *"Sir are you aware your neck is on backwards?"* he asked, noticing the sickening angle and protruding bone. *What a fucking sight, no wonder we all assumed he was dead.*

Rob didn't answer. Vince pointed out the bent twisted arm to Danny like he was casually picking what chocolate bar he wanted from the shop.

"Jesus fucking Christ, what happened to your arm?" Danny asked, without an ounce of sincerity but with the full hammy excitement of the campy B-movies he was drawing on as inspiration. He tried to suppress the laughter which was building inside him. *"My God, viewers I have never seen anything like it!"* He poked the spinal cord that shouldn't be on view, but

was.

Rob didn't flinch at the rough touch; he couldn't. Nor did he feel what would have otherwise been searing pain shooting through his body.

"And the smell," Danny faked, holding his nose like Rob was some decomposing corpse, rather than someone they'd broken an hour ago. *"A truly remarkable and terrifying creature."*

Jess got a good angle of both the neck and arm, zooming in for maximum effect. It looked like his head had detached from his spine, but Jess was sure he'd have been *dead*-dead if that had happened. *But it sure fucking looks like it.*

The arm looked just as bad, although probably less likely to cause immediate death than whatever the fuck was going on with his neck. There was surprisingly little blood, but somehow that just made the scene even more morbid. Jess loved it.

Some blood did spill from his mouth as his breathing further slowed. He tried saying something but it just came out as another whimper. He could move his eyes, but that was about it. Something in his brain must have told him the kids were responsible for his condition; it was obvious from his expression. The acceptance of death was mixed with disgust at the intruders hovering around him, but he was helpless to do anything about it as they continued to mock him.

Danny tentatively reached toward the dying man like he really was the walking dead and was going to suddenly snap his rotten teeth. He once again made a big show of it for the camera, pulling back several times and prodding various parts for a reaction, like he wouldn't be fooled. Eventually he slipped his hand into the man's pocket and pulled his wallet out.

He put the mic down to check the content. The first thing he saw was a picture of the man with, presumably, his family -- three kids and a wife. Danny showed the picture around the group, with each making some snide remark about a family member in order to kick the man while he was already down.

Vince suggested kidnapping the goofy looking fuck, referring to the bespectacled youngest of the three kids. Jess remarked on how Shane would love a go at the mum. He agreed, but also stated the eldest girl was looking pretty damn 'fuckable' too. As was normally the case, the middle kid got missed out, but they'd probably be grateful in this instance.

Danny asked the man if his daughter was legal, *not that it mattered,* but he didn't, and couldn't, answer. Had they fucked up his ability to speak? Wouldn't surprise Danny; everything else was broken beyond repair.

He asked again, cautiously leaning closer and still playing the role. "How old is she?"

The only response was a low, choking groan.

Not any fun if they don't take the bait. Wouldn't stop him trying though.

"You think your daughter will enjoy Shane raping her?" Danny persisted.

The man's agonized eyes told the whole story. *No he fucking didn't!*

"Blink once if you want us to pay her a visit, or twice if we should leave her alone."

The man seemed to struggle trying to make his eyes work properly, everything was fucked. He must have had no clue whether he was blinking or not. He could have blinked fifty times or zero times; no idea.

"No blinks means the whole family will get it," Vince added.

The part of the man's brain somehow still working must have known they were fucking with him either way; they'd do what they wanted and there was nothing he could do to stop them. "Yeah, my bro has his eyes on the dorky one," Danny laughed.

"Fuck you," Vince snapped, as his gaze flicked briefly in

Todd's direction.

Somehow, the man managed to blink. It must have been fucking exhausting and he might not even know if he'd succeeded, but he had. A second blink followed, after another strenuous effort. "We'll take it under advisement," Danny said, giving him a reassuring pat on his fucked up arm. A wasted gesture, much to his annoyance; the man was too far gone to feel much more pain.

Jess egged him on to continue the report. Danny checked the rest of the wallet first, finding nothing much exciting. The man's I.D. -- "Rob Clarke," he announced. "Must be the other guy's brother." Some cash he shared out between Shane and Vince. A bunch of credit cards and store cards. A winning scratch card for ten pounds that Rob hadn't got round to cashing in yet, *and never would.*

Oh, well. Danny picked the mic back up and brought it to his lips. Back to business, as inspiration struck. He beckoned Shane over. *"Doctor Evans is a world renowned zombie expert who just happens to be here on the scene at the exact moment the outbreak began. What luck!"*

Shane reluctantly joined him, trying to keep his eyes from making contact with the dying man's. He was having mixed feelings; threatening to rape his wife and daughter was one thing, but staring someone you thought you'd killed in the eyes was an entirely different proposition, and one Shane wasn't quite ready for yet.

"Is there anything you can tell us about this particular brand of zombie Doctor Evans?" Danny enthusiastically asked as he tilted the mic towards Shane, giving him an encouraging nod and grin. A pat on the back too with his charming smile infectiously making Shane smile as well, helping him get over another spate of stage fright.

"Well...He was dead." Shane stated, to Danny's overly-animated cartoony nods. *"But now he's alive."*

"Stunning insight from the world celebrated multi-award winning author of Zombies, the Dead Live. And its sublime sequel, Zombies, the Dead Don't Die." Danny mugged more to the camera much to Jess's and Vince's amusement.

Shane shrugged, knowing he didn't exactly nail that.

"Glad those improv classes are paying off," Jess teased.

A fresh round of blood spluttered from the man's mouth, along with an awful cry that would have made even the most cold-hearted bastard feel something, so, naturally it made Jess laugh.

Instinctively, Shane grabbed his head, bringing it briefly up in his massive hands before cracking it hard against the floor underneath, putting an end to his misery once and for all. This time he was *dead*-dead, and there'd be no coming back, despite Danny's mock book titles.

Danny stared, stunned, before shifting back to his reporter character full of energy and enthusiasm. *"Ladies and Gentlemen, the heroics of Doctor Evans are here for all to see! As the zombie lurched forward to take a bite out of this intrepid reporter, the doc sprung into action and used his expertise to put an end to the zombie apocalypse before it could even begin."* His stupid grin and cheesy persona grew. *"The world owes him."*

He signed off, much to the delight of Jess, who looked like she wanted to fuck him right there on the corpse, and was seriously considering it.

Shane stared at the dead body. The first time he 'killed' the man, it had been an accident, albeit one with the full intent to cause plenty of harm. This time, however, he knew exactly what he was doing, instinctive or not. He brought the man's fucked up, already broken head down with enough force to know that would be that. He was surprised he hadn't ripped the head clean off, giving how loosely it was already attached. Either way, he was dead, never to return.

Shane could persuade himself it was a mercy killing, and on some level it was, but there was more to it. He *wanted* the guy dead. It was no act of mercy. If anything, he was upset the guy was still somehow holding on. The more he thought about it, the more he wished he'd already been dead; him being alive had robbed Shane of a big moment in his life. One he'd soon corrected when he smashed that melon-fucking-head against the floor causing more blood than there'd been in the initial attack. *Another bonus.* Shane was more a gore and tits guy than psychological damage, so wanted his own horror scene to look as fucking messy as Hell. *It sure does now.*

Danny gave Shane another encouraging pat on the back, taking his silent contemplation as some form of guilt. "It was him or me, buddy," he joked.

Jess's eyes were full of questions. She wanted to know everything. How did it feel to kill a man? Could he tell the exact moment his life was gone? Did he feel powerful? Remorse? Excitement? Guilt? Horny? Confused? Anything? Nothing?

Shane just continued to stare. He wasn't a big thinker like Jess, and hadn't really given much thought to how exactly *the moment* would feel. Thinking back on the incident, though, his overriding feeling was one of pleasure. In fact, he was a little hard. Not quite full mast, like when he stuck his cock in Bev's mouth after pissing over her. Or when he thought about raping Elle. But not far off. Killing was quite the turn on. He knew Jess would understand, but kept it to himself. His fate was now sealed. He was a killer, and he fucking enjoyed it.

So, who'd be next?

Why?

Adam wept uncontrollably hearing the cruel death of his older brother. If a part of him had hoped Rob was still alive before, there was no doubt in his demise now.

"You bastards," he mumbled, wishing the true anger he felt was reflected in his voice, but he'd just taken too much of a beating and the gag was still partially in place. He'd barely regained consciousness when he witnessed the killing. He wanted to scream and curse, or more importantly put a stop to them and protect his family, but he couldn't do any of that. He was tied to the fucking chair, still bloody and broken.

His leg was a fucking state, and might even need to be amputated with the severe damage. His sides hurt, probably from some kind of internal injuries. His head was pounding and concussed. A pool of blood and vomit had gathered at his feet; he didn't even remember being sick, but didn't doubt for a second it was his own. In all likelihood, he didn't have long to live himself, but he wasn't willing to accept that yet, not while these ruthless cunts were still in his home.

"What'd you call me?" Vince strutted towards him like he was the fucking man and Adam was some scum who'd insulted his good name.

He gave Adam a sharp, stinging jab in the face, which sounded wet as it broke Adam's nose. Clearly buoyed by Shane's recent chance to shine, Vince was ready for his moment, and selected Adam as the target of his pent-up rage.

"I'll be back for you," he told Adam with a nasty grin plastered across his mug. before disappearing into the kitchen.

"Where the hell is he going?" Jess asked.

Danny shrugged his shoulders, *fuck if I know.*

"You ready for the next part of your interview?" Jess asked Adam, like they were at a news station.

No hint of them holding his family hostage, or having just broken his nose… or killed his fucking brother! The living room may as well have been the green room. She handed Danny the camera before checking her hair was still neat and her makeup still looked good.

The adrenaline of watching Shane kill had mixed with the pleasure she felt causing all the torment and chaos this evening. Her panties were soaked, and she considered taking a brief break in proceedings to let Danny bang the fuck out of her on the Clarkes' bed. Ever the professional, though, she decided the show must go on, for now.

She retook the mic as Danny framed her, licking his lips, with his erection bulging through his trousers, *clearly he was thinking the same.* He nodded towards upstairs with a lustful smirk, but she waved it off, mouthing, 'after this,' and one-hundred percent meant it.

She was as ready to burst as he was.

Shane took a position beside Danny with his attention flicking between the definitely dead man in the entryway and the tearful family in the kitchen. Elle was on the floor with her eyes closed, either still knocked out, or scared unconscious after Jess had threatened to cut her tits off. Bev was sucking back tears. The little lad Todd was crying too, and looking at Shane like a pleading puppy.

That wasn't going to work on him. He was a stone cold killer now. A real fucking man! Maybe in the past, the kid could have got to him, and possibly even reminded him a little of himself before he met Danny and the gang, but not any more. Shane had crossed a line which meant there was no going back, nor did he want to. The next stage of his life had begun.

Jess was ready to roll when Vince returned. He carried a metal toolbox in one hand and a pair of gleaming garden shears in the other. Danny and Shane couldn't help but laugh while

Jess rolled her eyes. *Boys will be boys.* He dropped the heavy toolbox on the floor, almost knocking over a light stand before showing Adam the shears with a maniacal smile spread across his cruel face.

"What are you going to do with those?" Jess asked.

Vince's face lit up. "You know exactly what I'm going to do with them!"

"I'm still interviewing him," she scolded.

"But..."

"No buts. Plus, this one's mine," she told Vince, running her finger under Adam's chin in an inappropriately seductive manner.

"After?" Vince bargained.

Jess had no intention of giving Adam to Vince but needed to keep things moving. "Maybe," she lied.

Vince gave Adam a psychotic look to let him know if it was up to him he'd be cutting him into little fucking pieces by now, or worse, sticking the fucking shears down his throat.

Something had definitely snapped inside Vince's already volatile and demented mind, and it was clear for all to see. The problem for the Clarkes was the others didn't care about Vince going a little nuts; it would be entertaining. They'd actively encourage it. As long as it didn't mess with Jess's shoot.

Adam looked away. He tried to turn his head to see his family, hearing Bev's and Todd's sobs behind him, but they were out of view.

Jess leaned towards him and took off his gag. "No shouting or screaming, or I'll send Vince over to your boy, with the toolbox. Nod if you understand."

Adam nodded. "I love you Bev. I love you Elle. I love you Todd," he said. Tears streamed from his eyes, stinging his busted nose and bruised face.

The tears, however, weren't from the immense physical pain

he had suffered; they were for the love he had for his beautiful family, and the regret for them being in this position.

"What? No more begging for your life?" Jess taunted, collecting a few tears from Adam's cheek with her fingers. She sucked them in front of him.

Adam didn't respond.

Bev tried saying the words back, but her gag had been put on extra tight after Shane stuck his dick in her mouth. Her eyes told the whole story, but Adam couldn't see them. He knew, though. Todd tried too, and a few muffles of sounds broke through, but Adam couldn't hear them. Again, he knew. Elle kept quiet on the floor, still out of it. The front of her shirt was ripped apart, showing her skinny body underneath. Blood continued to trickle from her mouth, where two of her teeth used to be. Despite her unconscious and beaten state, she also knew her father's true love for her.

"You all ready?" Jess addressed, ignoring the emotions pouring through the Clarkes. This was her time, not theirs. Their pussy feelings could wait.

Danny nodded and counted Jess in as she went full reporter again.

"The technical difficulties have been sorted and we now return with our live feed to Mr. Clarke," she began. *"He's just received the terrible news that his brother has died for a second time in the same attack! Mr. Clarke, how does it make you feel to know your brother died twice at the invaders' hands?"*

"Fuck you," was all he could mutter. His head hung low so the camera couldn't capture his reaction. His voice was soft, but with some venom behind it. He knew what was coming and had said his goodbyes. Adam didn't want to play their vicious childish game anymore.

"I'm sorry, Mr. Clarke, I didn't quite catch that over the sound of

your little boy's fingers about to be chopped off." Jess nodded to Vince, who snicked the shears with utter delight.

Adam lifted his head, his voice resigned. "Why are you doing this?" he asked, hoping the answer would be sufficient enough for them to leave his boy alone.

Jess gestured Vince to stay put, much to his growing disappointment, and Todd's relief. He'd wet himself again upon hearing what was about to happen, but no-one noticed as the smell of piss was already rampant.

"That wasn't the question, Mr. Clarke."

"I feel like you ripped my heart out," he replied, stumbling over the words as he tried to spit them out through his missing teeth, busted lip, and bruised jaw. The broken nose wasn't helping either, or the blood dripping into his mouth. He'd used what was left of his composure to tell his family how he felt about them.

Jess turned to the camera. *"Well, we haven't got to that part quite yet,"* she said with a light-hearted chuckle, like it was all good natured fun. *"And how did you feel about Shane sticking his cock in your wife's mouth after he peed on her?"* She asked it like it was a perfectly reasonable question. No malice or spite, just an honest question from a dishonest hack reporter.

Adam shook his head, unsure how to possibly answer.

"Oh right, you didn't see that," she announced in mock surprise. *"Awk-ward."*

Shane broke into a smile at the memory, while Bev could still taste his manky dick and rancid piss in her abused mouth.

"Why us?" Adam asked once more. At this point it may not have mattered, but he still wanted to know.

Jess pondered his question for a second, piquing Danny's curiosity, as he also wondered if there was an answer. They'd all assumed it was random. That Jess just found a family who fit the profile of the type of victims she wanted, and away they went, but her delay now suggested it wasn't quite that simple. She was hiding something. A reason? A why?

"Do you want an exclusive scoop, Adam?" Jess asked, breaking character as she leaned towards his face, her ass in the air and her lips almost touching his ear. She gave Bev a wink from the provocative position like she was about to mount her man in front of her and there'd be fuck all she could do about it.

"Tell me why you've done this to my beautiful family." Adam kept his words steady and understandable. The near death he felt moments ago had briefly stepped aside so he could hear an explanation.

Jess looked to Danny, a vulnerability printed on her face which he'd never seen before. He wanted to ask her as well now, but instead zoomed in to capture the revelation. She was breathtaking, and Danny would do anything for his girl, but his mind was racing. What had she held back from him? From all of them?

She retook her standing position beside Adam. She nervously fiddled with her hair before staring directly down the lens of the camera into the dark souls of whoever would be watching.

"Breaking news in the Clarke home invasion story; we've just discovered the attack wasn't as random as first suspected. In fact, Mr. Clarke himself, and his slut whore skank of a wife, were specifically targeted."

Jess composed herself for the big reveal while Danny took a step forward, angling the camera in tighter on her.

"It appears the reason for the attack is that Mr. Clarke is a piece of shit father who abandoned his daughter before she was born to take up with his cunt wife. Now that daughter is out to teach him a fucking lesson he'll never forget."

Her voice notched up in the evil department as she hit the

last few words. She dropped the mic to the floor so she could address Adam properly, while the boys stood stunned.

Danny wanted to give her a hug, seeing the emotion break in her face. Vince, on the other hand, was annoyed this wasn't completely random. He'd liked the idea of this just being any old house. It felt more dangerous, and evil, and fucking badass. Shane was worried they could now be linked to the family. He thought the idea of it being random was so they couldn't be fingered as potential suspects. He thought to the unused mask lying in the back of the van and all his DNA spread over the kitchen floor.

Adam looked confused rather than shocked by the revelation. *His wife did too.*

"I'm not your father," was all he could manage to say as he tried to process what the fuck was going on.

It almost came out as a laugh; it was so unbelievable. But he didn't want to rile this delusional psycho up further. *Have we been attacked because of mistaken identity? Was Rob killed over a misunderstanding? Because that's some fucking bullshit right there!*

"You are," Jess coldly told him, like it was an undisputed fact.

Bev tried speaking from the kitchen behind them but the gag stopped her words once more.

Jess directed Shane to take her gag off. "No screaming; Vince still has the shears," she warned, and meant.

Shane removed the tea-towel from Bev's mouth, allowing her to gulp in some much needed air and give her a moment to compose herself. "Adam's not your father," she told Jess like she was being a silly little girl.

"He is," Jess sharply replied, not impressed with Bev's tone. *Bitch should be grateful for the un-gagging.*

"I don't understand," Adam stated. Not in a million years could this horrible mouthy vicious obnoxious cunt be his

71

daughter. "Who's your mother?" he asked, hoping the mistake might set them free despite the damage which had already been done.

Danny was curious where this was going too. He had a bunch of questions of his own, but for the moment kept the camera aimed at the pair of them, wishing they could bring Bev into the living room to make the unfolding drama easier to shoot. Instead he had to take liberties with the zoom control, as she looked just as perplexed as Adam in the background.

There was no hint on Bev's face of believing Adam had another child, or that he'd been unfaithful to her at any point. They'd been together for what felt like a lifetime now, and not once had he shown the slightest sign of infidelity. Despite several of her friends having cheating spouses, it was something she never had to worry about with Adam. He was a loyal, caring, loving husband. She had her man's back one-hundred-percent, and and was mystified by the harlot's accusation.

Jess hunched beside Adam. The report seemed to be over for the moment but Danny kept recording. He liked the barrier of the camera; it made everything feel more cinematic and daring. It wasn't that he couldn't face real life and used the camera as a shield; quite the opposite, in fact. He felt like he was documenting real life. Not that bullshit of going to work and catching up in coffee shops, but the real drama of life. The meat of the matter. The real hardships and evils. Whether Jess wanted this moment on film or not hadn't really occurred to him; he just knew he wanted to capture it.

"My mum's Sarah Whitmore," Jess finally answered.

Revelations

"Huh," Bev scoffed, before spitting the remaining piss from her mouth and trying to rid herself of the taste of Shane's foul cock. "That explains a lot."

"And what exactly does it explain, you fucking home wrecking whore?" Jess's coolness faded. Her playful wickedness was replaced by sheer malice and utter contempt. Rather than teasing and enjoying the hurt she was inflicting, now she wanted to carve her fucking name in Bev's stomach and burn her in front of her kids. Rage had taken over.

Even Danny sensed it. He liked it when Jess was all fired up; she was a fucking handful and he enjoyed that, but tonight was meant to be fun. Depraved disgusting murderous fun... but fun nonetheless. For the first time since they'd broken in to the Clarkes' home, Jess didn't look like she was enjoying herself. Something inside her switched at Bev's mocking tone.

Jess reached into the toolbox. She rummaged through it with the look of an addict searching for a hidden stash, until she found what she wanted -- an electric hand drill. She looked in Bev's direction, who quickly got the message and stifled her scorn. Jess pulled the trigger on the drill to make her intentions fully known, but there were no batteries. If anyone wanted to laugh at the mishap, no-one did.

Sensing just how fragile Jess's sanity was, Adam jumped in, trying to take the attention away from his endangered wife.

"I'm not your father," Adam repeated in a neutral voice. He wanted his message to be clear, but he had no intention of winding the girl up the way Bev had. He knew she was ready to explode.

"My mum hid me from you when you left her," Jess replied, tossing the useless piece of shit drill back into the toolbox. She was still sneering at Bev, but was more interested in what Adam

73

had to say. "When you left her for that skank." She gazed at Adam for any signs of guilt or regret.

"I never dated your mum."

"You don't need to date someone to fuck them," Danny intervened with a chuckle. He got a 'shut the fuck up' look from Jess which made Shane smirk and Danny mouth 'sorry.'

"I never slept with you mother; I barely knew her," Adam continued.

"Yet you both immediately knew her name." Jess snapped.

"Cos she's a fucking psycho that made our lives hell," Bev spat. "The apple didn't fall far from the tree, I see."

"Bev, please," Adam interposed before Jess really did fly off the handle and plunge a drill into his wife's neck. He needed her not to antagonise the crazy bitch further, not with their kids tied to chairs and Vince holding a pair of shears he was itching to use.

He studied the young woman. His head was held up now rather than hanging. The pain had to be put to one-side for the moment, knowing he needed to handle this right. He sensed there still could be a chance for them all to get out of this alive.

"Jess ..." he began, then politely follow with, "Is it okay if I call you Jess?"

"If you're not ready for daughter dearest, then Jess is fine," Jess cutely responded, but there were still daggers in her eyes.

Danny rested a hand on her shoulder as he passed the camera to Shane and quietly told him to keep rolling. He slid his hands around Jess's waist, comforting her while she interrogated her old man. He didn't mind her flying off the handle and butchering the fucker, but he wanted her to enjoy the moment, not be upset. He didn't want this asshole stealing her thunder. This was her evening, not his. If he could call a time out he would, but Jess wasn't the type of girl you ever told to calm down. *That would cost me my balls.*

"Your mum and I were never a thing," Adam said. "I was just starting out with Bev when I knew her."

"That's not what she told me."

"What did she tell you?" Adam asked, still keeping his tone under control despite his own rage surging through his body at what these punk kids had done.

"That you cheated on her. Abused her. That she'd become your piece of meat on the side when Bev didn't spread her whore legs."

Adam shook his head.

Bev had to hold in her laughter. She was about ready to burst. Despite the cruelties, and her brother-in-law lying dead by the front door, that was some funny shit. She was practically going red in the face holding it in.

"I can see you smirking, bitch," Jess told Bev. "Vince, take the kid's pinky."

"No!" Adam shouted, hurting his throat in the process. His eyes implored Jess to hear him out.

She put her hand up, denying Vince his fun once more.

Quite frankly, Vince was getting sick and fucking tired of all this family drama *Jeremy Kyle* bullshit and wanted to carry on what they were here to do. *If I don't get to cut someone soon...* He shot Danny a look, but Danny gestured for calm. Unlike Jess, Danny had some degree of control over his deranged brother, but that too was reaching its limits. Vince swung his arms irritably, knocking a light stand to the floor. He picked it back up without anyone saying a word as the bulb inside began to flicker.

"Your mum liked me, back in the day," Adam began, getting Jess's attention back from Vince's tantrum. "She wanted us to be together, but I wasn't interested."

"You calling Jess's mum fugly?" Vince barked. Adam ignored the rabid idiot.

"I was her crush, I guess. Honestly, I barely knew her. I'd seen her around a little but that was it."

"Then why'd she tell me you're my daddy? Huh? Why she tell me that you used to fuck and dump her any chance you got? Slap her around if she threatened to say anything to your cunt face wife over there?"

With great effort, Adam shook his head. "I don't know why she told you that. Clearly, she wasn't right in the head," he told her in all earnest.

"What'd you say?" Jess broke free of Danny's loving grip and angrily dove back into the toolbox.

Vince smiled when she pulled out a hammer. Finally.

"You know that to be true more than I do," Adam continued, trying to keep his composure. "Like I said, I barely spoke to her. Just some pleasantries here and there. But I know you've seen it."

Despite him keeping his voice calm and honest Jess cracked the hammer down hard on his right knee. Shattered his kneecap instantly upon impact as his leg crumbled. Adam howled in pain while Bev screamed at Jess to stop.

"What did I say about screaming?" Jess yelled.

This time, Vince didn't wait. He darted towards Todd and grabbed his hand. Still tied up, Todd had no chance to avoid him. Before any more could be said. Vince snipped off the tip of Todd's pinky with the shears.

Like a knife through butter. Should have tried cutting his whole fucking hand off, Vince thought.

Todd screeched into his gag, desperate to hold his mangled finger.

Bev's face was aghast. Jess stared her down, daring her to scream again, as Vince poised the shears around the base of Todd's index finger. The blade accidentally cut him a little in the process as the boy struggled ... *That will learn him.*

It took everything she had left, but Bev kept quiet as her husband and son both raved in agony. Todd's index finger stayed attached for the time being, but the accidental cut had already dug through a fair portion of it. Vince reckoned he could probably tug the rest off, and wanted to try. *Maybe later.*

"That's what I thought," Jess told Bev, still trying to provoke another outburst.

Bev had learnt her lesson, as the blood squirted from where the tip of her son's pinky finger used to be. Todd started to hyperventilate. He wasn't a kid used to pain. He'd never been in a fight and didn't play sports enough to fall over and scrape a knee, although that wouldn't have prepared him for what he was feeling now.

"Please help him," Bev begged.

Vince picked up the kettle. "You want me to cauterise the wound?" he laughed.

"Try taking deep breaths, honey," Bev told Todd, ignoring Vince's cruelty. She desperately wanted to hold her little boy. Comfort him. Rush him to the hospital and get the tip of the finger reattached. Then fucking bludgeon Vince to death with the kettle.

Vince crushed the finger tip under his boot, ending any thoughts of reattachment. "Oops."

What a cunt.

Todd got his breathing back under control and avoided choking on the gag, but whether that was a good thing or not remained to be seen. For the moment, he was soldiering on.

Bev couldn't take her eyes off her baby boy until Jess readdressed her beaten husband.

"Did you rape my mum, Adam?" Jess plainly asked. bringing the attention back to her as Adam sucked in the pain of his shattered knee.

Like Todd, he wanted to hold the wound. Cradle the

damage. But he was also still tied. The latest pain brought back everything he'd pushed to one side as well. His whole body felt on fire, while simultaneously he felt cold and could sense everything slowly shutting down inside him. He couldn't endure much more.

"Did you abuse her? Use her? Fuck her and dump her at your leisure?"

"No," he muttered back.

"Was she just a fuck toy to you? A plaything. Any hole's a goal?" Jess sternly questioned, and meant every word. She wasn't trying to get a rise… scarily for Adam this was a legit line of questioning in her warped mind.

"I never slept with your mum. Ever!"

"You didn't fuck her behind the cafe where she worked?"

"No."

"Cum on her face and not let her wipe it off?"

"What?"

"Slap her when she refused to rim you?"

"No. Of course not!"

"You didn't bang and choke her in her apartment before peeing on her and never coming back?"

"What the fuck are you talking about, you crazy cunt?"

Wham!

A second blow with the hammer destroyed Adam's remaining kneecap, much to the delight of the three lads, who cheered at the horrible crunching sound the connection made.

Danny and Vince egged her on while Shane did his best to capture the vicious assault on video. He had to zoom out, struggling to follow Jess's sudden strikes as she smacked the hammer against his legs over and over, albeit with not quite as much gusto as original the kneecap shot. Shane did manage to capture the pain and agony on Adam's face as his body went into shock.

"Your mum lied to you!" Bev screamed from the kitchen, desperately trying to stop them hurting her husband. "She used to stalk him. We had to get a restraining order. That's why we both knew her fucking name. I don't know who your father is, but it's not my Adam."

She wanted to say a lot more. Wanted to be cruel to the girl. Tell Jess her dad was probably some fucking deadbeat meth dealer her mum used to visit, because that was a million times more likely than it being Adam, but she had to restrain. Her beautiful daughter was knocked out on the floor with half her clothes ripped off. Her little baby boy was in tears, missing part of a finger. Adam was practically fucking dead, which was one step away from her brother-in-law, who was actually dead. She wanted to give Jess everything she had, verbally annihilate the callous cunt, but couldn't.

"They have a restraining order against her?" Vince questioned, worried about even more connections to the household, and their chances of being caught. *Not that Dad won't get us off any charges.*

"They're lying," Jess told him straight.

"Doesn't matter either way," Danny reassured. "Was twenty years ago. They ain't linking any of us to this."

Adam mumbled through the searing pain, getting Jess's attention.

He's a resilient bastard for someone wearing a blood-soaked Elmo T-shirt, Danny considered, somewhat surprised Adam was still even alive.

"This is just a misunderstanding," Adam slowly told her with each breath a struggle. "Your mum has remembered things wrong." He sounded ready to drop at any given moment. He continued his plea though; had to, for his family. "I'm not your father. I never slept with her. I have two kids and a wife and I just want them to be safe."

"You have three kids," Jess corrected.

She turned her attention to Todd, who was still whining about his missing and squashed finger tip in the kitchen.

"You want another big sister don't you Todd?"

The brat didn't reply.

"What about you Elle? Need a big sis to help sort out your fucked up pathetic love life?"

She waited for a response, but Elle still lay on the kitchen floor with her eyes tightly closed.

"She still out of it?" Jess asked.

Vince gave Elle a kick. No response.

"Pussy," was all Jess could say, seeing the young lady not moving. Her attention returned to Adam who was bleeding out fast and trying to somehow keep himself from dying.

Everything hurt, and his body really did want to completely shut down. Survival mode at this point meant just letting himself die so he could escape the unbearable pain, but he had to protect his family.

"You know my mum killed herself last year?" Jess coldly told him. Danny squeezed her shoulder gently. "She told me about you the night before she slit her wrists."

She leaned in closer to Adam. Right in his face.

He could have head-butted the wicked bitch if he had the strength.

Jess considered her words as tear formed in her eyes. "Why would the last thing she ever tell me be a lie?"

Adam didn't know the answer. He didn't know why the crazy bitch lied to her daughter about their non-relationship. None of it made any sense. And now her equally insane offspring was in his house, hurting his family, killing them! All because he hadn't been interested in going out with her twenty odd years ago. *What the actual fuck!*

But how could he tell the unstable psycho her dying mum's last words were complete and utter horseshit? A nonsense fabrication because she didn't get her way? Why the fuck was he still even on her mind after all this time? He'd moved on from the nothing; why the hell hadn't she?

His mind was too foggy from the damage caused to his body to work out a way to delicately put it. Given some time, and a fucking notepad and diagrams, maybe he could explain that her mum was full of shit and desperately needed help she clearly never got, but he didn't have that time.

Maybe he'd eventually even feel guilty she'd held on to this for so long. He hadn't thought anything of knocking back her advances in the day. There was nothing between them. No connection. No spark. She was most definitely not the one. He hadn't even known her full name until they had to get the restraining order! He'd certainly never fucked her and put a kid in her! Before a few minutes ago she'd been the furthest thing from his thoughts imaginable. If Jess hadn't mentioned her, he would have gone the rest of his life without remotely remembering her.

Is that why she said what she did? He had no answers... but Jess was waiting.

*

Elle heard every word of the crazy bitch's made up story. She knew her dad was telling the truth, because he was a terrible liar. It was one of the reasons her mum trusted him without a shadow of doubt; he couldn't tell a lie if his life depended on it.

Plus, he was a caring wonderful father with a pure loving

heart. If Jess was *his* daughter, he'd have looked after her too. But no fucking way was that cunt his daughter. Not a chance. There was nothing of her father inside that psycho's dark soul. Nothing that could have allowed Jess to order Vince to snip Todd's finger off, or break her face and threaten to cut her open.

Elle had feigned being knocked-out in order to give herself more time to undo the bonds. The fall from the chair had helped loosen the ropes further, after the water from the bottles had softened them. The kick in the face hurt like hell, a pain which Elle had never felt before, although her broken fingers were close. She'd managed to keep her busted mouth shut afterwards. She'd closed her eyes and kept them that way, even when Jess threatened to cut her tits off.

She been inadvertently saved by her uncle's dying groan. Even in death, he'd been looking out for her. That brought tears to Elle's eyes, but they weren't spotted. Everyone was too wrapped up in the ridiculous accusations of Jess's lying mum.

All this had given Elle the time she needed to untie the ropes, escape the zip-tie, and set herself free.

Free?

With her hands free of the zip-tie and rope, Elle reached up to her mum's restraints. Bev's weren't quite as loose as Elle's, and no way was she going to be able to pick them free. She needed a knife, or the scissors on the kitchen counter, but any big movement would attract attention from the gang of intruders who were currently on the verge of killing her father.

Todd continued to cry at his missing finger tip, unaware of Elle's freedom, while Bev looked straight ahead to her husband being tortured, trying not to rush Elle as she felt her daughter's delicate hands doing their best.

Elle had no choice but to go for the scissors. She slinked back to the floor when Vince took a fleeting glance in her direction, but risked half-opening her eyes when he resumed to laughing at her dad's pleas for them to leave his family alone. She saw Shane still doing a horrible job behind the camera, and Danny urging Jess to torture her father more and more as she continued to demand answers. She clearly wanted him to tell her to her face that her mum was a fucking liar, and then she would probably kill him. Time was running out.

Checking that no one else was looking in her direction, Elle slowly and quietly made it to her feet. Her broken fingers throbbed, while her mouth felt puffy and full of cotton. She knew a couple of teeth were gone, which freaked her out no end, but it was a problem for another day. *If we survive this one.* Her whole body ached too, but she couldn't think about that.

The only thing that mattered was freeing her mum. Her eyes betrayed her for a second, spotting their phones. They'd be a risk to grab, but calling for help was also high on the list of things to do. Her mum's pleading face suggested freeing her first, so that made Elle's mind up.

Vince spotted Elle just as she snatched up the scissors.

Caught her red-handed. He wasn't overly worried or concerned by her escape; more excited at the prospect of her being free. They could go back to having some fun after all this family bullshit.

He gave Danny a playful tap on the shoulder, drawing his attention to Elle standing there like a deer in headlights. Then Vince darted forward as Elle got the scissors around Bev's zip tie. She snipped the restraints free and yanked at the rope she'd loosened just as Vince reached her.

Instead of going for Elle, he threw a sickening haymaker at Bev, who still had her arms behind her back. His fist exploded against her unprotected jaw, knocking her the fuck out before she could do a single thing to help.

Elle leapt for the phones on the table, but couldn't get a grip as she'd used her damaged hand, not thinking in her moment of desperation. The whole gang laughed at her poor choice, while Danny blocked off the escape route to the front door and Vince circled behind her, preventing any possible way of reaching the back door.

He was too close for her to try for the phones again, despite him daring her to. She was free, but trapped between them. With no other option, Elle darted towards Danny, before ducking to the side and up the stairs like some dumb teen in a slasher flick. *But what other choice do I have?*

She tripped climbing the first few steps, jamming her broken fingers on the staircase as she put them down for support. *Ouch!* That elicited more laughter from below, and Elle turned to see who was chasing her.

No one was. Instead, Jess had grabbed a saw from the toolbox and was holding it to her dad's throat.

"Don't you dare take another step, sis," Jess told her, with a wicked grin spread across her devilish face. She had her swagger back, alight with joy again, like this was the best possible scenario.

Danny retook the camera from Shane so he could expertly capture the confrontation between the alleged estranged sisters. Shane started towards Elle but Danny nodded him back. *Let's see how this plays out.*

Vince uprighted Bev and used the spare rope to retie her hands, having run out of the zip-ties. Bev was mumbling something but the words made no sense. In all likelihood, she was still out of it. Vince slapped her a few times to see if he could bring her to, but he really did clobber her and the lights were still out. He licked her face just to fuck with her, but she didn't even react to that. *Damn, I caught her good.*

"You going to come back downstairs and stop fucking around?" Jess asked, with her voice practically purring.

"Let him go," Elle screamed, hoping a neighbour would hear.

Jess dug the saw into Adam's neck, drawing a fresh dribble of blood from his already ravaged body. "How about you keep the noise down, bitch?" she suggested.

"Run Elle," Bev mumbled. Her jaw stung and her words sounded weak and pathetic, but she meant them. All her faculties may not have been firing, but her motherly instinct needed her daughter to be safe.

"Yeah, Elle. Run," Jess dared, as she dug the saw even further into Adam's neck, drawing more blood as the rip teeth made easy work piercing his skin.

If she applied any more pressure, it wouldn't be long before she caused permanent life-ending damage, and Elle knew it as she helplessly watched. The teeth of the saw were begging for a vein and Jess was teasing it. Adam tried retracting his throat but was in no state to manipulate his body. He was at Jess's mercy; just the way she liked it.

"Please," Elle prayed, as tears flooded her face.

She didn't have a clue what to do. She so badly wanted to run. Get the fuck out of there. Find some help. Hopefully all in time to save her family, but at the same time she was frozen to the spot. A helpless little girl in a hopeless situation. The scissors she didn't realise she was still carrying slid from her left hand. Her mangled right hand went on barking in pain. Even uttering the plea hurt as her mouth felt like shit.

How did any of this happen? Earlier in the evening, Megan hanging out with a cheerleader was the absolute worse thing to ever happen in Elle's life. Now, her uncle was dead, and the rest of her family were being held hostage by a bunch of crazy assholes.

"Please," she said again, knowing that it would fall on deaf ears, but not knowing what else to do or say.

"You really are a pathetic little girl aren't you?" Jess mocked, seeing the helplessness in Elle. "Have you had to fight for a single thing in your life?" she asked in all seriousness.

Elle shook her head. Sobbed uncontrollably. She looked to her mum, but Bev couldn't offer any aid. She switched to her dad's resigned, bloody face instead. He tried to summon a comforting smile, one that suggested everything would be ok, but it didn't even succeed at a surface level. He couldn't even fully form the comforting smile he'd given her every single day of her life. That same smile she saw earlier in the evening, when he'd claimed the whole paint incident was just to cheer her up. She believed now more than ever that it was.

"You coming back down, or do I cut Daddy's head off?" Jess asked, like she was speaking to some brat who wouldn't go to bed, except her ultimatum didn't involve removing video game privileges.

"Do it babe, this is your moment," Danny urged.

His latest erection bulged inside his jeans. Seeing his girl hold a fucking saw to Adam's throat, ready to hack his head off in front of his family, was the hottest thing he'd ever seen in his life.

Might have to look into that.

She looked angelic with the smile across her face and the spark in her eyes, although he thought that probably wasn't the right description, as angels didn't decapitate people as far as he was aware.

"Please," Elle begged once more, although it was more a pitiful whine in Jess's ears. The soft, pampered girl seemed to be stuck on loop.

Fuck it.

Jess hacked the saw across Adam's throat, viciously tearing it open as the sharp teeth penetrated his soft skin with ease. He couldn't even hold his hands to the crass open gash as the blood cascaded and the last few gargles of life escaped his lips. Jess carried on sawing even after the throat was slit. Her intention was way beyond just killing him. She wanted his fucking head, and to teach the spoilt daughter a lesson.

Elle's screams couldn't leave her busted mouth as she watched the waterfall of crimson spilling from the perforated slit below her loving father's jaw. She watched in horror as Jess continued to saw away at his neck, struggling to get through the bone, but with a determined look on her face suggesting this was fucking happening; even if it took all night. She watched the murderous bitch's tongue slide to the corner of her mouth in concentration as she hacked at her dad's head after murdering him in front of her.

She couldn't move a muscle and was out of tears. They just suddenly stopped like she'd dried up, or they held no purpose anymore. What had happened was above the emotion tears could convey. She could hear her mum's muffled screams against the replaced gag and Todd's cries reach levels she didn't know possible even with his own gag stopping some of the wounded sounds escaping.

Everything felt in slow motion as the saw continued to cut across her father. Each slide back and forward dug further into his neck. His eyes had fallen back, mercifully. He was at least dead now, and didn't have to feel the jagged saw slicing through his veins and bone.

Bev was going fucking wild in her seat. The grogginess gone the second her husband's life was heartbreakingly taken. She bucked and thrashed and struggled with everything she had for freedom, but was no closer than she'd been the whole night. These murderous lunatics were fucking Boy Scouts when it came to tying knots.

Todd had closed his eyes, wishing himself away to some fantasy world where this couldn't possibly be happening. The gang of intruders hadn't noticed, or had forgotten their own macabre rules. Or they simply didn't care anymore, as they were having too much fun carving his father up, the saw continuing its arduous task of freeing Adam's head from his shoulders.

Danny moved around Jess, capturing every angle of the decapitation. Each strenuous slide of the saw across the throat was a chance for him to show his artistic side. The blood had stopped spraying like a hose and now leaked like Adam was a slaughtered pig hung upside down and being drained. *He simply has no more blood left to give.* Some had got on the camera, but Shane wiped it off for Danny each time like a good camera assistant.

Plenty had drenched Jess; she now resembled *Carrie* in her ruined prom dress. Except Jess wasn't the hero of this story, and she wasn't soaked in pig's blood. She took great pride in being the villain as she continued to hack away.

Vince was fucking howling with laughter, and stroking his cock, apparently just as turned-on by the brutally as his brother. *We really are alike*, except for the moment Danny had managed to keep it in his pants, as he had a job to do. Vince was ready to burst. His eyes kept flicking from the gruesome decapitation to the remaining two tied members of the Clarke family, deciding which one would receive his built-up spunk.

None of the gang had made a single move towards Elle. She simply wasn't a threat. Wasn't even worth considering in this magical moment, other than as an object of their laughter.

"I told you to get the fuck down here," Jess howled to Elle like the punchline of the funniest joke she'd ever told. "Look what you've done to our father" Tears of laughter streamed down her blood-soaked maniacal face.

"I was going to," Elle whispered, without thinking about the words or meaning to say them. It was like her broken mouth acted on its own as her brain wasn't there to help. Elle's mind had momentarily left her. Fight or flight? It had chosen flight. This was too much to deal with.

"This is on you," Jess coldly told her as the saw dug further into Adam's throat, making it a fair old way through the bone.

Then, Adam's head flopped back like a fucking PEZ dispenser as Jess nearly made it all the way though. Finally Adam could have seen his bound distraught wife behind him, only there was nothing remaining of Adam's soul to truly see. He had long since departed. Instead, she had to stare at his cold blank eyes where so much warmth once shone during the life they'd spent together. She had to watch as his head hung loosely from what remained of his neck at an angle no head should ever be.

All the thrashing, raging, and screaming stopped.
Jess had finally broke Bev.

She'd been a tough cookie up to that point. Despite everything they'd done to her and her family, the woman had continually fought against them and her ties, despite it being an impossible task. They'd beat the fuck out her husband, killed her brother-in-law, embarrassed and kicked her daughter, chopped one of her boy's fingers off, and pissed over her while raping her mouth, and she'd still shown defiance.

But now that fighting spirit was gone.

Bev stared at her husband's head as it fell to the floor with one final hack from the blood-thirsty saw. Cheers erupted from the triumphant home invaders at the splat it made, and Bev wished she was dead.

She wished her kids were dead too, so they wouldn't have to suffer anymore, or live with the image of what they'd just witnessed, for however little life they had left. There was no getting out of this. Their lives were over. Why didn't they stop toying with them and finish the job? She'd welcome the cold touch of the Reaper.

Live Man Hunt

Jess picked Adam's bloody head up from the floor, holding it in the air like a proud barbarian. A few remaining drizzles of blood and gore hung from the crudely hacked neck stump while the rest formed a messy puddle on the floor.

Swaggering to the kitchen table, Jess plonked the gruesome paperweight down next to the phones, mad-dogging Bev the whole time. She could see the fierce woman was broken and beamed at her achievement as she angled the gruesome head at Bev. *The cat that got the cream.*

Jess grabbed the individual phones from the table and slammed them against the floor one by one. She stomped repeatedly on each even if the tiles had already done the job, each breakage shattering any remaining possibility of help.

No one was coming to save them. They were beat. All were going to die horrible deaths. Jess just wanted to hammer home the point and break Bev further, *if that was possible.* She turned to Elle, wanting to further rub the salt in her wounds too, but she girl was gone.

"She make a run for it?" Jess asked the boys in a disturbingly nonchalant manner. *Drenched in my father's blood and terrorising his family without a care in the world.*

"Bolted upstairs," Vince replied, still tugging his meat, ready to fucking explode.

"Live man hunt?" Danny suggested.

Jess nodded her approval. "Live man hunt," she repeated.

Danny gave the camera back to Shane and suggested he head up to find her.

"Go with him Vince," Jess asked, as she eye-fucked Danny. "We've got some busy to take care off down here."

Vince let go of his raging hard-on, disappointed at not getting to cum yet, but excited at all the horrible things he could do to Elle. He grabbed a mic in one hand and retook the shears in the other as he gestured for Shane to follow him upstairs.

Shane just about managed to hit the record button in time.

"This is Vince Woods on the scene as we close in on the notorious runaway crybaby coward, Elle Clarke."

Jess and Danny both laughed their approval, but also hoped they'd hurry up and leave so they could fuck.

*

Elle burst into her bedroom and darted straight for the window. Locked. She found the key hanging from a hook alongside it and tried her darndest to jam it into the hole and unlock the fucking thing.

Every part of her body was shaking uncontrollably and her mind was fuzzy and checking out. No one should ever witness what she just saw. She was considered soft at the best of times, let alone dealing with insane bullshit like this.

And her dad… she couldn't think about it, yet, it was all she could think about. They sawed his FUCKING HEAD OFF! Elle didn't even know that was possible.

She turned the key and pried the window open, momentarily distracting her morbid thoughts, but the safety latches clicked in place and the window barely opened big enough for her arm. No way was she fitting through that small of a gap, and she didn't know how to release the latches. She remembered they were a pain in the ass and her dad always had to get her mum to do it. *Not ideal for escaping a fire,* Elle previously joked, but now something much worse had consumed her family.

"Fuck. Fuck. Fuck!" she screeched at the stubborn window. It didn't improve the situation. She considered trying to break it, but the glass was thick and she barely had enough energy to stand.

Plan B, (or C if you included the momentary thought of breaking the window.) Elle staggered to her closet and searched for a shoe box sitting beneath her clothes. She pulled out an old phone, which looked like a fucking brick compared to her current phone, but still wasn't an old enough model to be wielded as such as she contemplated hurling it at the stupid window. She held the power button down to turn the damn thing on but nothing happened. It had been years since she last used it. She rummaged around the box for the charger, while the image of her dad's head being sawn off played continuously in her mind. *Would it be there forever now?*

She wanted to close her eyes and wake up to this all being a dream, but she knew this nightmare was real, and time was of the essence. She could already hear Shane and Vince bantering on the stairs, doing their fucking moronic reporter impressions. Once again they were having a great time at Elle and her family's expense. Elle wished she had it in her to brutally kill the fucking lot of them, but she couldn't even open her damn window. She was a child, not a fighter, just like Jess told her.

Elle found the bulky charger as she heard the lads reach the top of the stairs. Vince continued taking the piss out her beyond the faux safety of her bedroom door.

"The escaped family member was last seen crying her eyes out and sucking her thumb, calling for her daddy as she headed towards her little girly bedroom," Vince mocked, before tripping on the top step her dad had always meant to fix.

"You ok?" Shane asked.

"Fucking keep rolling," Vince snapped back.

Elle had no lock on her door, and didn't have the time to charge the phone the little it needed before they reached her room. There was only one option. With the phone and charger in hand, she exhaustedly hobbled from the sanctuary of her bedroom to the bathroom, the only room in the whole house with a lock.

"What a moment for all our viewers. The fugitive caught live on camera," Vince told the camera, being careful not to trip again as he walked backwards with his mug looking directly at the lens.

He gestured Shane to follow as they slowly made their way to the bathroom, milking the scene for everything it was worth. Shane's camera work was all over the place, shooting the floor, roof, and bedroom doors. Anything but Vince. They were both having too much fun to notice.

They reached the bathroom door and he turned the handle, ready to do whatever he pleased with her.

Locked.

*

With the boys upstairs hunting her mousey 'sister' Jess and Danny were finally alone, if you didn't count Bev and Todd, which they didn't.

The lust in Jess's eyes was unlike anything Danny had ever seen before, but he understood; he felt it too. Torturing and killing this family was the ultimate foreplay. He was absolutely certain his prick had never been this stiff in his whole damn life. He could hammer fucking nails with it.

And Jess seemed to be so wet she was dripping through her panties, although it could have also been the copious amount of blood which had splashed over her. Either way, Danny needed to be balls deep in her moist cunt straight fucking now.

Jess stripped from her bloody dress, removing her bra and knickers as she approached Danny. He undressed just as quickly. Neither could hold out a moment longer. Jess had needed this from the moment Shane killed Adam's brother, and the itch intensified tenfold when she got to do some killing herself. She hadn't even had time to contemplate taking her father's life, and what that meant, but fuck it, there'd be time for reflection afterwards. Now she needed to get her freak on.

She stop just short of Danny and stood naked beside Adam's headless corpse with a sinful glint in her eyes. She once again glanced at Bev, jamming a couple of her fingers into her glistening pussy. Bev was looking in her direction, but whether she was registering anything going on around her since Adam's beheading was an entirely different matter. The lights were on, but no one was home.

Jess scooped up a handful of blood and gore from the stump where Adam's head used to rest before it found its new home on the kitchen table. She lubed her cunt with the butchery and draped herself across Adam's lap. Grabbing hold of his broken legs, Jess aimed her ass in the air, positioning herself to be spanked like a naughty child ... but that wasn't the punishment she desired.

Danny didn't need asking twice. He rammed his granite-hard cock deep inside Jess's bloody pussy and instantly emptied his pent up blue balls. He'd barely got his hungry dick inside her before shooting into her guts and letting some of it fly over her thighs and ass while the rest landed on Adam, further desecrating his corpse. He'd never come so much in his life, *didn't know I had it in me.* He almost wanted to apologise for the premature ejaculation, but it felt too damn good, and Jess was right there with him anyway.

She gushed everywhere like a fucking sprinkler system going off. The second his throbbing cock touched her blood-coated pussy lips her entire body began to shake. She let out a primal satisfying scream as orgasm after orgasm hit, digging her claws into Adam.

This was the peak of her sexual life, and she knew it. No way would she ever feel this horny and satisfied again. It defied all logic and reason. She thought she was going to die of dehydration, so much fluid squirted out of her. It coated Danny's dick and balls as well as dribbling over Adam, mixing with Danny's cum. The guy just had the best three way of his fucking existence and wasn't alive to appreciate the incest.

Jess further collapsed into Adam's lap, laughing at the ridiculous orgasm; and the absurdity of the situation. Danny was in hysterics too as he bent over and kissed his murderous gorgeous girlfriend while she laid naked and bloody across her decapitated father's lap with half his viscera and Danny's cum inside her still sopping cunt.

"Love you," he whispered tenderly into her ear.

"Love you too," she smiled back at her flawless man on this most perfect of evenings.

*

Elle had locked the bathroom door and moved the freestanding shelving rack in front of it. Various shower gels and shampoos spilt to the floor and the flimsy racking didn't offer much extra protection, but anything that could slow them down even a little was useful.

With the shit barricade in place and the bathroom door locked, Elle plugged the charger into the wall and began trying to power the old phone. The damn thing wouldn't even turn on, so she needed time for it to work its magic, but whether she had time or not depended on the assholes fucking around outside the locked door.

*

Vince stood proudly outside the bathroom door, mic in

hand, doing his best to look like a professional reporter, while Shane held the camera as steady as he could. For once he was doing a half decent job of it.

"*We've tracked the fugitive to this location and are just mere moments away from returning her to her rightful place in the kitchen.*" Vince sniggered at the last part of his clever double meaning joke before second guessing himself. "Did that sound right?" he asked.

Shane had been too busy holding the camera steady for the words to register but Vince didn't wait for a reply anyway.

"Let me try it again," he told Shane, who nodded in reply not entirely aware of what Vince was talking about.

Both got set in their positions once more as Vince loosened up a little and brought out his finest devilish grin as he mugged for the camera just like his older brother had done during the zombie apocalypse. Oh, how he wanted Danny's charisma, but sorely lacked it.

"*After a daring escape and gruelling chase we've tracked the fugitive to this very bathroom and are just moments away from recapturing the bitch and having our way with the slut.*"

Both laughed as Vince showed the camera the shears he'd brought along and was still desperate to use. Sure, he'd cut a fingertip off with them, so they'd seen *some* action, but he had much wilder ambitions. He tried the door again.

Shockingly, it was still locked.

*

Elle heard the knob being twisted and rattled but the door held firm. After some muttering from beyond the door that she couldn't quite make out, the door shook as a shoulder rammed into it from the other side.

The crap barricade, and surprisingly decent lock, both held

firm. It wouldn't last, as a second shoulder barrage splintered the door inwards, but she still had some time.

Her eyes scanned the small bathroom, looking for anything she could use as a weapon. She regretted dropping the scissors in her daze, but she'd had other things on her mind at the time. *Like my fucking dad getting decapitated!*

The shelves propped against the door offered little in the way of weaponry, and the bathroom floor wasn't inspiring either. The best it had to offer was a wicker basket full of laundry.

The only thing she could remotely consider a weapon was a pair of nail scissors resting beneath the bathroom mirror. They paled in comparison to what she'd dropped, but they had to be better than a towel, or a bottle of shower gel.

She grabbed the little scissors, shadowing a few stabs with them. She'd hadn't had the courage at any other point in the night to fight, so why she thought he could now was anyone's guess. But, having seen what happened to her father, she knew there was no other way out of this. She had to at least try.

Vince's reporter voice echoed though the door as Elle stood with the makeshift weapon in her good hand. *"We have you surrounded. Unlock the door and come out quietly. You've got nowhere to go."* He went quiet for a second and she heard Shane sniggering. Then he added more. *"Plus our dicks are hard and we need something to put them in,"* he laughed.

Shane's booming laugh joined Vince's as Elle shrunk back against the far wall at the thought of those two bastards raping her.

Then her phone sprang to life as the once upon a time familiar start up tone chimed.

Elle Fights Back

"I thought Jess destroyed the phones?" Shane asked, part curious, part concerned the bitch was calling for help. The last thing he wanted was to end up in jail for murder, or for their night to be ruined by some rat.

"Fuck." Vince shouted before ramming his shoulder harder against the door.

Shane was about to offer his help when Vince booted the fucking thing a couple more times out of frustration and practically put his foot through the wood. After, he jammed his shoulder into it again and violently knocked it open, sending the weak barricade to the deck.

Success!

Vince saw Elle with the phone but she hadn't started dialling yet. The old thing was taking forever to go through its startup routine.

"Caught red-handed, again," he told Elle, like she was in trouble now. *As if she hasn't been all evening.* "Give me that."

Elle shook her head as Shane captured what he could see of the exchange from beyond the doorway. The bathroom was small and Vince stood in the entrance with Elle further back almost sitting on the bathtub. There definitely wasn't room for Shane in there.

Vince kicked the flimsy - and completely useless - rack aside as he barged his way towards Elle, but got his leg stuck in-between its thin shelves. *Or maybe not so useless after all.* As he stumbled forward to within arm's reach of Elle, she struck.

With a shout of aggression she hadn't shown all evening, Elle drove the point of the tiny scissors into Vince's face. The blow ricocheted off his cheekbone and she ended up sticking them in his shoulder. The scissors weren't big enough to cause any severe damage, but they stung like a motherfucker and left both a cut on his cheek, and a mark on his shoulder. Not Elle's intended target, but she wasn't done yet.

She stabbed him again, in the upper arm, causing Vince to drop the shears into a pile of displaced toiletries. Vince got himself more entangled within the flimsy shelves and stumbled to the floor as Elle stabbed at him for a third time. This time she cut his right palm as he raised it in defense.

"You cunt!" he yelled.

That just made her stab him in the palm again, drawing more blood as the wound opened up.

She also used the opportunity to start dialling as the startup process finally finished and the emergency call button was on display, but Vince grabbed her legs from under her before she'd even punched in the first nine. *About how the night had gone.*

Elle fell to the wreckage underneath, scraping her elbow on the rack and dropping the tiny scissors, but she just about kept hold of the phone.

Shane considered springing into action, but carried on filming instead, chuckling away at Elle briefly besting his mate. Her advantage hadn't lasted long, though, as Vince looked ready to go medieval on her.

He snatched the phone from Elle's hand and seized her skinny leg with his other. He squeezed her ankle tight, digging his fingers in, and causing her to cry out loud enough for her mum to hear downstairs. Vince slapped Elle's open mouth, stinging her already busted lip, and loosening another tooth.

His attention returned to her wounded hand, which she held tightly against her chest. He pried her good fingers apart and crushed the broken ones in a vice-like grip, causing another satisfying scream from his homemade final girl. His mood had quickly picked up seeing the pain jolt through her scrawny body, and catching a glimpse through her ripped shirt only widened his smile.

He untangled his feet and made his way up. Vince showed Elle the chunky phone one last time before tossing it in the toilet like he was an NBA all star, even held a pose for a second afterwards for those with the benefit of flash photography. Relaxing from the pose, Vince checked the damage to his own hand while Elle whimpered on the floor. The bitch had pierced the skin, and if they went for takeaway later every handful of chips would sting, but he'd live.

As for her, though?

Vince slapped Elle across the cheek with the back of his hand, hard enough to hurt, but restrained enough not to knock her the fuck out. He wanted her to feel the same pain he felt as he pawed at the mark on his cheek, then she'd feel a hell of a lot worse. He pulled the mic from his trousers and turned back to Shane, who was still filming from the doorway like this was all part of the show.

"Bitch cut me," he told Shane, who nodded like he saw, because he did. "Do I still look pretty enough?" he asked with an awkward wink.

"Mate, you never did," Shane howled.

"Fuck you," Vince bit back. It was hard to tell whether he was joking or pissed off.

Shane was used to it, so just continued to chuckle and film.

Vince straightened himself up and looked into the camera as Elle lay at his feet, defeated once again. *"It's been a long night, folks, but the runaway whore has been apprehended."*

Shane tilted the camera down to Elle who continued her mewling. He zoomed into her ripped top, determined to capture the goods. Vince helped as he bent over and tore the top further, then yanked at her bra until one of her small tits was on display.

"Nice," Shane approved.

"After her daring escape, the little slut made it to her bedroom and retrieved a secret phone that she'd stashed like the deceitful cunt she is.

Retreating to a nearby power source, the whore barricaded herself in the panic room."

Shane smirked at the idea of the bathroom being a panic room. Vince struggled to keep it together too. He composed himself before continuing his embellished twisted tale.

"There, she tried to call for help before being heroically stopped by yours truly. A brief fight ensued and the dangerous fugitive managed to stab me multiple times." He showed the ugly cuts on his palm and shoulder to the camera, as well as pointing to the scratch on his face.

Shane crash-zoomed into all of them, which would make for horrendous viewing should anyone ever watch the report. He settled back on Vince.

"But, despite her savage attack, the slut was stopped in the nick of time and her phone destroyed, reinstalling order to the invasion, and making sure this little cunt will be eating dick sandwiches for the rest of her short life."

Vince smirked at Elle before bending down. His hand ran over her stomach, resting on her exposed little breast. She tried pushing him off her, but Vince knocked her hand away.

"We're going to fuck you straight, you fucking mug-runcher." Vince coldly told her. The bulge in his jeans tried to press against her prone body. Luckily for Elle, the loose shelving provided some projection, but Vince's intentions were perfectly clear. He leaned in closer whispering in her ear so Shane couldn't hear. "Then I'm gonna fuck your little brother too."

Elle struggled to buck him off but Vince was just too strong. She screamed and clawed, but he gave her another slap, unimpressed with her efforts, while Shane laughed at her pathetic attempt to fight. He hadn't heard whatever Vince whispered, but he liked the reaction it provoked.

Neither of them noticed during their laughter Elle

rummaging through the rubble, or the dropped shears within her reach.

"This is Vince Wood successfully signing off, and about to unleash his cock." Vince went to produce his dick for the camera, wanting to show off his stiff, waiting fuck stick that he was about to ravage Elle with, *in case they didn't get the innuendo*, when he felt something press against the front of his jeans.

His own pair of shears, blades open in a V with his bulge in the middle.

"Don't fucking move," Elle told Vince through her tears. She sounded exhausted and hurt. Mentally scarred and broken. Her whole body was in pain as she used her destroyed fingers to hold the shears, but none of that mattered.

She couldn't let them dominate her like this anymore. It was time to stand up for herself, unless she wanted to become their plaything, or next murder victim. Neither of which she did. Plus, there was Vince's threat towards her brother, which she knew the sick fuck meant.

"I could easily knock them out of your hand." Vince did his best to remain cool and calm, but inside he was worried little Vince's days might be numbered.

"You want to try?" Elle challenged, with a steel she didn't know was within her. She closed the shears further, shrinking Vince's balls back into his stomach. The metal scraped against his zipper.

Shane smirked, not believing for a second she would do it. Vince, on the other hand didn't want to take the chance.

"Drop the mic," she told him. He did. "Now put the camera down," she barked at Shane.

He shook his head.

Elle tightened the shears further. Vince could practically feel the blades, cold and sharp, against the shaft of his rapidly shrinking dick. He thought she'd cut right through his jeans and have an all access pass. The shears still had splatters of blood on them from the little kid's finger, and Vince didn't want to add to the mess with his dick and balls.

"I said put it down!" Elle reaffirmed.

Shane smirked at her.

"Dude," Vince protested at his friend's stubbornness.

"This little girl ain't gonna cut your dick off."

Vince stared at the shears, still dangerously close to his cock. Part of the denim already looked shredded. *Nope.* He definitely wasn't willing to chance it.

"Plus, it makes great viewing," Shane added, with a smile that made Elle want to throw up.

This really was a fucking game to them. A bit of fun. Some banter. She wanted nothing more than to cut this asshole's cock off, but that wouldn't save her mum and brother from the others.

In one swift movement Elle stood upright and moved the shears from Vince's crotch to his throat. The asshole sighed in relief, which made Shane burst out laughing.

"What?" Vince chuckled back, although still nervous of the blades. *Better his throat than his dick though.*

"You think this is fucking funny?" Elle yelled, sounding like an angry yapping puppy.

Even with a pair of shears held to her brother's tormentor's throat, she still couldn't come across as threatening. Just didn't have it in her, and they knew it. But she had to try. She had to make them believe she could kill this piece of trash. Part of her did believe maybe she could. That was the part she needed to focus on.

"Back away from the door," she told Shane, who this time did follow orders - *because it made for great footage.* She held the shears as close to Vince's throat as she could. Her weak arms and fragile hands tried their best to betray her, to fall to her sides or lose the grip, but Elle kept herself in position ready to slice this motherfucker if he tried anything.

For his part, Vince went along with things. He felt sure he could overpower her, but in the back of his mind he replayed how he'd nearly sliced Todd's index finger off when the kid made a sudden move. She could accidentally kill him with those fucking things. It had been a dumb mistake for a kid, so as an adult, Vince should know better. For the moment, he'd tread lightly.

"That bitch isn't my sister," Elle said, trying to keep the situation moving during an awkward silence.

She needed them to be thinking about anything other than trying to overpowering her. She could *probably* slice this asshole's throat if things got hairy, but the big bastard would kill her right after. Again, her plan was to save her mum and brother, rather than take revenge on Vince.

"We don't care if she is or isn't," Vince answered. He tried to sound tough, but a little nervousness crept into his voice.

"We're here for the fun, not the family reunion," Shane reaffirmed.

Elle nicked Vince's chin with the blade, causing it to bleed.

"Fuck," he muttered, staring daggers through Shane, knowing his smartass answer caused the cut.

"Next one's a vein," Elle threatened. Her eyes told Shane she might actually mean it too, so he held off any more sarcastic reply.

"Head to the stairs," she ordered. "Now."

Hostage Negotiations

Danny watched from the kitchen as Shane carefully reversed down the stairs, pointing his camera back up. He was curious how things with the girl concluded now his mind was back in the game, and his balls were empty.

He'd wiped blood from his dick with a tea towel, and cleaned himself some more with a splash of water from the sink before sliding his trousers back on. He'd need a good shower when he got home, but the night was still young.

Jess stood next to him, naked and covered in gore, looking like she'd taken part in some kind of satanic sacrifice. The big smile plastered across her face suggested it was as the priestess with the ceremonial dagger rather than the damsel in distress. She'd always been comfortable with her body, but even if she hadn't, she couldn't give a shit. Everything in her life felt too good. The night had been perfect. Unforgettable.

Bev remained in her catatonic state, staring towards her husband's decapitated head on the kitchen table. The head looked ugly and bloated, nothing like her husband's sweet loving face, but underneath the blood and torment it was him. At least, part of him. The rest remained in the living room, tied to a chair, battered and destroyed, covered in all manner of bodily fluids from the assholes who'd taken him from her.

Todd took to tightly closing his eyes again while snivelling on the chair. The top of his removed pinky hurt like hell and his body was starting to go cold through blood loss and shock. His index finger was held on by a thread and it was lucky he couldn't see it because it looked fucking disgusting. Some of the blood had dried around the cuts, while plenty stained his hand and mixed with the urine beneath him. He'd wet himself again since his dad's death but there was no embarrassment anymore, just sheer terror at the savagery he'd witnessed. Seeing his

LEGO destroyed angered him; witnessing his dad's head being hacked off broke his little innocent heart.

Shane made it to the bottom of the stairs. He flicked his eyes upwards gesturing to Danny something was going on. Danny craned his neck and spotted his little brother held hostage by the whiny girl who barely looked strong enough to hold a bag of sugar, let alone his badass brother captive.

"What have we here?" he questioned, like the three of them had been up to no good. Her ripped open shirt added to the illusion.

Elle descended the stairs with the shears opened around Vince's neck, ready to prune his fucking head off. Vince looked nervous, but wasn't making a big deal of things. More a look for help, rather than outright pleading for it. He was aware one slip on the stairs meant his throat would be sliced open. Vince was clumsy at the best of times, so had to be extra careful at the worst of times.

"You get any good footage?" Danny asked Shane, ignoring his baby brother's life threatening predicament.

"Loads," Shane replied, equally nonchalant. He backed away further, camera capturing the quandary as he aligned himself with Adam's desecrated carcass, catching a whiff of wild sex as he stood there.

Jess smiled at Elle as she finally noticed what the fuck was going on. She was almost proud of her sister for showing some balls. Although, like Shane, she didn't for a single second believe Elle could kill Vince.

"Get away from my family," Elle ordered as she reached the bottom of the stairs. She wanted to say plenty more, pissed with them chatting about the quality of their 'footage,' but her priorities were rescuing her mum and brother, not scoring points arguing with these fucking degenerates.

"Not happening," Jess replied, accompanied by a simple

shake of the head.

Vince was crestfallen at the reply, but understood none of them truly believed the scared young girl would do anything to him. *Hope they're right.*

Jess wiped blood away from her mouth, probably got there when she was bent over daddy dearest, and grabbed the spare microphone sitting next to Adam's head; left there after the weather report. Shane spun the camera to face her and she fell straight back into reporter mode, like she wasn't butt naked covered in blood from head to toe with cum and guts dangling from her sopping pussy.

"We're here live at the Clarke residence as the hunt for fugitive Elle Clarke has taken a dramatic turn"

"Stop!" Elle yelled wanting to close the shears around Vince's neck and show them she wasn't fucking around.

He could feel it too as they drew nearer, desperate to spill more blood.

But no way was Jess going to stop. *"Our reporter on the scene has been taken hostage by the deranged dyke and is currently being held at shear point."*

"I said stop!"

Elle looked to her mum for help, but Bev was checked out, her eyes still on Adam's head, barely aware of her baby girl in front of her, or the evil blood-drenched wrench next to her.

Todd opened his eyes, hearing his sister's voice. He was quietly cheering her on as the siblings made contact. Elle nodded to him that everything was going to be ok, just as her dad had tried doing for her earlier. It wasn't convincing, but Todd appreciated the gesture.

Danny dove into one of the duffel bags they'd left beside the kitchen table and pulled a pistol from it with a big grin on his face. The Glock belonged to his father and he'd packed it for emergencies. His brother being held captive was such an emergency. He may have been acting aloof, but no way did he want any harm to come of his bro. Vince meant the world to Danny, and this little cunt wasn't going to end him.

Shane panned the camera between Jess, Danny, and Elle, unsure where to point it until Jess started speaking again.

"Due to the serious nature of the situation, we've flown in special hostage negotiator Danny Woods. All round hero, badass, and brother of the hostage. Folks, business has picked up."

"Step away from my family," Elle again demanded. The sight of the gun made her whole body stiffen but she couldn't lose control. She tried to keep herself hidden from the gun using Vince as a meat shield.

Holding him tighter only made his dick hard again. Apparently, his life being in danger was a turn on to Vince, *like everything fucking else!*

Danny didn't aim the gun at Elle; however. Instead, he pointed it at Bev's head. "You want your mum looking like him?" Danny negotiated, as he quickly flicked the gun in Adam's direction before settling it back on Bev's temple. This close up she could very well end up looking like Adam's headless corpse if the gun went off. "Or maybe you want your brother looking like that?" He grinned, swinging the handgun at the crying youngster.

Jess addressed the camera. *"Negotiations have begun."*

"What have we ever done to you?" Elle cried, knowing how hopeless her position was.

"Nothing," Jess answered, blurring the lines between her reporter persona and herself. *"Unless you count our dad being a scumbag father."*

"He's not your fucking dad!" Elle screeched, much to Jess amusement.

"He is." Jess answered back while licking some of Adam's

blood from her arm.

Vince couldn't help but stare at her naked beauty while Danny wanted another go. Despite the tense situation, all eyes were on Jess rather than the weapons.

"Just let them go…" Elle's voice gave up on her mid-sentence, knowing these fucking psychos were just going to laugh at her.

"You want to trade?" Danny asked, back in his negotiations role.

Elle nodded.

Shane continued to film it all to the best of his limited ability, swinging the camera between Elle and Danny, while making sure to linger on Jess as much as possible.

"Give me back my brother, then we can talk." Danny started.

"Release my family first," Elle countered.

"Not how it works."

"*The negotiations are intensifying,*" Jess butted in.

"Shut the fuck up," Elle angrily shouted at Jess.

"You speak to her like that again and I'll put a bullet in this bitch's head," Danny sternly warned her.

"And I'll kill your brother." Elle quickly replied, and tried to show in her face she meant it.

Danny studied the look trying to work out if she did mean it or not. "With garden shears?" he questioned, like it wasn't possible.

Elle hoped it was.

"*Negotiations appear to be moving forward,*" Jess reported, daring Elle to get shitty with her again.

Elle didn't take the bait this time as she stared at the gun pointed at her mothers head.

"Please?" she asked Danny, hoping his family was as important to him as Elle's was to her.

"Ok," he reluctantly replied. "We can trade."

BANG!

The bullet exploded through Bev's head, practically ripping her skull in half. Her eyes already looked lifeless, but the bullet was the final nail in the coffin. She died without a gasp or a whimper, not that she would have had time for either. Her destroyed head flopped forward.

The bullet, fortunately for Todd, slammed into the wall just beside him, the through-and-through barely missing his face. The same couldn't be said about skull fragments and gunk from his mum's brain, however, as they drenched the poor kid. He may have wished the rogue bullet had connected and ended his life; now both of his parents were gone and he was wearing half his mum's head.

Elle could only let out a miserable 'nooooooo,' mystified by what just happened.

He'd said they could trade, yet now her mum had joined her dad in the afterlife. Just like that. One loud bang and the most important person in her life was no more. Her whole body ached physically and emotionally as she stood staring at her dead parents. Both in sight from her point of view. One missing his head, the other's blown apart.

Danny shimmed up to Todd next. "Your brother for mine?" he offered as the trade.

It didn't matter. Like her mum after the death of her father, Elle had checked out.

Vince grabbed shears from her before Elle dropped to her knees, defeated. She hadn't even heard the offer, and if she had, she'd have known it was bullshit. They had no intention of trading. Of letting any of them go. They were going to kill all of them.

Vince kneed her in the side of the head for good measure

before rejoining the gang. She was lucky he didn't cut her fucking head off right there and then, but he wanted to prolong her suffering after the shit she'd pulled. Shane gave him a high five as he approached Jess.

"That just leaves you for the kill, Vinny boy," Jess suggested, nodding to the shears in his hand and clearly the path to Todd.

Finally, Vince thought, as he made his way to the youngster.

"I'm pretty good at this hostage negotiations shit. No one got hurt," Danny announced, before glancing at the dead mother beside him. "Well, not the hostage anyway," he followed, giving his brother a pat on the back.

"You're a natural, babe," Jess reinforced, and gave him a big hug.

Elle remained comatose on her knees as Vince approached Todd.

"Time to die, little man," he told the kid, like the Devil himself had made an appearance.

In Todd's eyes, they were all the Devil. All demons sent from hell to plague his family. His life flashed before his eyes as Vince raised the shears. His thoughts shuffled from the life he wanted to lead making monsters and movies, to the holiday he'd been so excited to go on which had just been weeks away. He thought of his father's goofy smile, and his mum fussing over his hair. *Should have just got the haircut.* He thought of his sister trying to protect him and how he wished he could have told her he loved her and it was ok, she could come in his room.

He tried to get the words out but Vince blocked the opportunity.

Vince jammed the garden shears down the kid's throat and tried his hardest to open them. Todd couldn't even cry in pain with his mouth full of metal. Vince couldn't get the blasted shears to fully extend. Blood flowed from Todd's mouth as the insides of his throat ripped and the metal tore at his teeth. He choked on the blades and blood, his body convulsing.

It may not have been the spectacular *Handyman* death Vince wanted to cause, but it was fucking cruel, and did the trick.

He left the shears in the kids split dead face. "Guess it's harder than it looks," he joked, to a round of laughter from the rest of them.

They turned to see Elle's reaction but the front door was open and the girl was gone.

"Guess that's a wrap," Jess announced, unfazed by the disappearance. She looked to the camera Shane still held.

"This is Jess, signing off after a long, brutal, and thoroughly successful night. Hope you all enjoyed it? I know I did." She blew a kiss to the camera as Shane stopped the recording and Danny gave her a hug.

"Right. Grab the gear and lets burn this fucking place to the ground" Jess told the group as she turned the oven on.

Exactly Ten Years Later

There was always some nasty shit going on in town of late, but it was rare Jess got the phone call to cover a murder.

Normally, that was Andrews' job, but he was already busy with another one. Two in one night; the news was going to be dramatic today.

Just the way I like it. It's what she got in the business for. She couldn't turn down stories about local fairs, pet shows, and the cost of living, but she was here for the violence and brutality. She wanted to report the assaults, arsons, and rapes, and got her share, but Andrews got the juicier homicide stuff, having been with the news station longer. So, when Jess got the call to report on a murder, she was absolutely fucking delighted, even if she couldn't show it.

The news van pulled up outside the taped off garage. A small crowd had already started to form, which the police kept back. Three cop cars were on the scene, along with a forensics van. They weren't fucking around.

Jess hoped she'd still be able to get some good pictures of the crime scene, but it depended on who was working. Her ex, Danny, always let her get the good stuff if he was on duty, but most of the other officers were a little more by the book and strict. *Guess they have to be as their dad isn't the chief superintendent.*

Danny wasn't there, but another officer she knew, Holmes, was. He had a somber expression on his face as Jess approached the tape and was let through after flashing her reporter's badge to the officer guarding the entrance.

"You been told much?" Holmes asked as she approached him.

Jess shook her head. The call had been last minute when it was clear Andrews couldn't make it. Jess was told it was gruesome and messy, and that's all she needed to know.

Holmes put his hand on Jess's shoulder like he was comforting her. Jess smiled back, confused by the gesture and carried on inside with her cameraman in tow.

They weren't kidding about it being gruesome. The workshop floor at the mechanic's was a river of blood. It looked overkill. Like someone had been butchered but there still wasn't enough blood so they shipped in a couple of extra barrels to make the crime scene really pop.

She was led to the toilet out back where the victim rested, although rested was definitely not the right word. He'd been drowned in a toilet filled to the brim with piss. Plenty had splashed over the side and mixed with an over-abundance of blood. *What a way to go.*

The victim was a big man, his melon head almost too large for the toilet, but some determined killer had jammed it in there and drowned the fucker.

It hadn't occurred to Jess when she arrived, as she hadn't seen him in six years, but the victim was without question Shane.

She'd spent enough of her teen years hanging out with him to recognise him anywhere, even with his head stuck in a toilet and his body slashed to pieces. Someone had done a real fucking number on him. His intestines hung from his ample gut and his hands were missing their fingers. If she'd lifted his head from the bowl, she'd have noticed his eyes had been taken too, but it wasn't her job to touch the body, just report it.

Jess stared at her mutilated former friend, her thoughts instantly going to Danny and how distraught he was going to be.

She heard the whispers from the officers about a possible gang hit; if that was the case, then Vince would be involved too. He was the power in these parts - unofficially of course - and Shane was still one of his best friends.

Whoever had done this was going to pay. If a rival gang had gutted Vince's mate and drowned him in his own piss, the streets would run red, and Jess would have plenty more murders to report.

The forensic officer and photographer hovered around the scene doing their thing while Jess tried to gather herself for the report. It wasn't often she was quiet and stopped in her tracks, but seeing Shane like this had done it.

Her cameraman, Ben, questioned if she knew the victim, seeing her change in demeanour. He knew she wasn't fazed by the gore; it had to be something else. Jess could only nod. She didn't get a chance to explain.

"Shit!" Holmes muttered behind them as he tucked his phone back in his pocket.

He mumbled something to a few fellow officers before heading towards, Jess just as her eyes fell on a sticker stuck to the ceramic bowl. Out of place amongst the blood, gore, and piss, and the general aesthetic of the garage, was a *Hello Kitty* sticker.

"We just got word the victim at the other murder scene is Vince," Holmes quietly told Jess.

It wasn't news she was meant to know, but Holmes knew her history with Danny and his brother. *Well, some of their history.*

Holmes held back his own reactions himself. He had no love for Vince and his brutal gang of thugs, but Danny was his friend, and this was going to be a rough fucking day with two of the most important people in his life viciously murdered.

"The chief's on the warpath," Holmes added.

All the officers knew what Vince really was, and so did his dad, but blood was blood, and whoever took the Chief Superintendent's son was going to pay dearly. The officers may have turned a blind eye to Vince's crimes, but couldn't to his death.

Jess dialled Andrew's number. He picked up immediately, clearly having heard the connection himself.

"Shit," he muttered over the phone. "Got ourselves a gang war uh?"

"Is there a sticker by Vince?" Jesse asked, her voice cold and perturbed.

No one was used to her being spooked. The woman was unflappable. She had a stronger stomach for this shit than any of the officers or other reporters. *Although it was rare the victims were her friends.*

"A sticker? Let me check. They haven't let me see the bodies yet. Is a fucking slaughterhouse here. Someone took out the whole gang."

Jess's trained eyes flicked around the room searching for more clues while she waited for his answer.

The sticker made no sense; it couldn't be what she thought it was. But then, Vince and Shane dying on the same day made no sense either.

Gang warfare was the obvious answer and the one everyone would arrive at, but the officers weren't privy to information she knew. They didn't know what was so special about today. They didn't know what had happened ten years ago on this very night.

Fuck, Jess herself barely remembered. It seemed like a lifetime ago.

The four of them had grown apart since then. Vince went off the rails afterwards, getting a real thirst for the blood, and ended up a gang leader within the city and surrounding area. Danny had followed in his old man's footsteps and became a police officer, of all things. He was good at the job too. He still had a wild side, but took it out on criminals rather than the innocent. He was making a documentary about the force in his spare time just to keep those old creative juices flowing. Shane, as far as Jess knew, had just carried on being Shane. He worked at the garage, drank too much, ate too much, and hung out with his friends when he could. The last time she'd seen him, he had that same loveable dumb expression on his face he always had.

Andrews' answer snapped Jess from her reverie. "There's a fucking *Hello Kitty* sticker where Vince's dick used to be, apparently," he told her, half bemused and half disgusted. "Have you got one too?"

"Yeah. A *Hello Kitty* sticker on the shitter," she responded on pure instinct. She needed to end this call and contact Danny right away.

"The Hello Kitty Killer, or the shear killer if you count what's stuck up his ass..." she heard Andrews laugh as she hung up on him and began to dial Danny's number. He didn't answer.

"Fuck," Jess yelled, causing a few glances in her direction. "I have to go," she told the bewildered cameraman while sucking in some deep breaths and trying to compose herself. She felt like she was going to faint.

"What? We haven't even started recording yet," Ben replied, uncertain of Jess's bizarre actions. Sure, her friend was dead, but this was still unlike her. She was a professional.

She ignored him and headed outside to the fresh air and the van, pulling out her phone and making another call.

"Honey, is everything ok there?" she anxiously asked as soon as her husband answered.

He, too, was caught off guard by her tone. She sounded... scared? That wasn't the woman he married. *She was fearless.*

"Everything's fine," he told her. "You ok?"

"I'm coming home right now, Glenn. Pack some clothes for the girls; I want us to go away for the weekend."

"What?"

"Just do it," she snapped. She caught herself for the moment, annoyed with her own hard tone. "And Glenn, I love you." He returned in kind, although still bewildered.

Jess turned to the cameraman. "Drive me to my house," she demanded.

He nodded, still not having a clue what spooked her either. No one would ever believe him back at the news centre if he told them Jess was acting this way.

*

Jess burst through the door to her beautiful home, instantly noticing the quiet. Her house was never quiet. While adorable, her two little girls were absolute chatterboxes who never shut the hell up, and they were so fucking loud too.

But the house was quiet as a grave. Eerily so. She wished she'd accepted Ben's offer to come inside with her after he dropped her off. Jess pulled out her phone and started to dial the police; something was definitely up.

She was knocked the fuck out before her fingers even touched the screen.

*

Jess awoke zip-tied and roped to a chair. In front of her, her husband and her two little girls were also bound and gagged. Both daughters, the six year old and the four year old, were in tears, crying for their mummy behind the tight gags. Her husband looked terrified, both at the situation, and of his wife.

His eyes flicked to the TV, where an edit of the fateful night ten years ago played. It showed Jess reporting naked, drowned in blood, with a decapitated man at her side, and a sparkle in her eye.

How? was all Jess could think.

That tape was her pride and joy, but it was a secret to

119

everyone and kept under lock and key. The only people who even knew of its existence were the ones who'd been there that night, and none of them knew where she kept it now. Nor did they have copies.

She watched the footage she'd masturbated to so many times play out now on the big screen. It was less erotic with her young daughters and bewildered husband in the room.

There was a Hello Kitty sticker stuck to the top corner of the telly; that was different too.

Part of her wanted to comfort her daughters, or try to explain to her husband about the video. Make up some bullshit about it being a horror smut movie or something. *Didn't you know your wife used to be an actress?*, she'd joke.

But instead her thoughts were purely on the only person who could have done this, no matter how improbable it may have been. The girl who'd escaped that night, never to be heard from again.

"Elle?" she asked aloud.

Jess, like everyone else, had presumed she was dead. The local police even put the blame on her for setting the fire, as she was the only body unaccounted for.

"The things she'd done to her family first… they reported, knowing very fucking well fires didn't cause decapitations and gunshot wounds. Jess had fingered herself to that report many times, too. Talk about being able to have your cake and eating it.

But now…

"Hey sis," came a soft voice from behind her.

Jess tried to twist her head, but couldn't get a good look until Elle padded past her, bare-footed and not looking anything like the feeble little girl she remembered.

She looked filthy, head to toe, like she'd spent the last ten years in a dumpster, but she smelt of strawberries as if she was fresh out the shower. Her hair was a dirty blonde and her skin looked rough. Jess couldn't get a look at her face as she approached the TV but noticed she'd packed on some muscle.

Mercifully for her girls' sake, Elle turned off the tape showing Jess and her buddies killing her family.

But then she replaced it with a more recent recording. A single static shot showed Elle ripping Vince apart and fucking *eating* him!

Andrews hadn't told her that.

She'd castrated the poor fucker too, and at some point had shoved a pair of rusty shears up his asshole. Then fully extended them! His eyes were gone and his teeth snapped crudely off. He was barely recognisable, but Jess knew it was Vince.

Bodies from his gang lay everywhere. It was the bloodbath Andrews had spoken of. Most had bullet holes in their heads. None were left alive.

The tape flicked to Shane. It was a crude cut, but Elle hadn't had the time to edit the video in a professional manner the way Jess had. Through another static shot, Jess watched as Elle battered the fuck out of Shane like a ravaging animal. She was unrelenting, with the bigger man not standing a chance. She tore into his guts and dunked his head in the toilet, drowning him in the pissy bowl. Then she went back for more tearing up of the corpse, bringing it to the state Jess saw it in.

A final cut showed Danny without any arms or legs, wiggling around crying on the floor, with his cock stuffed down his throat and a Hello Kitty sticker stuck to his forehead. He was begging for his life but his pleas were ignored.

Instead, Elle finally put several bullets in him, and ripped him apart using the recently-made holes. She jumped up and down on his head after, until just a bloody pulp remained, then smeared the camera lens with his blood.

"Please," was all Jess could say, the fight drained from her as she saw her former friends destroyed.

Elle left the recording running on loop as she circled to Jess's family, twirling a brand spanking new saw in her hand. Jess previously hadn't noticed it; now it was all she could see.

"No… please… please…" she begged as Elle stood behind her youngest daughter.

She finally got a look at Elle's eyes. They were as black as night. Pitch black. They didn't look real. The life that used to be in them had been taken, and Jess could guess when.

Her face wasn't contorted with anger and vengeance, however. Quite the opposite, in fact. It looked almost playful as she put the saw to Jess's young daughter's neck and began to hack off her precious little fucking head.

The End.

Books by Stephen Cooper

Abby Vs The Splatploitation Brothers: Hillbilly
Farm
Near Death
Blood-Soaked Wrestling
The Rot
Not Four Children
Ensuring Your Place In Hell
Hack

Short Stories Available on Website or Godless

State Of My Kitchen
Hillbilly Mom
There's An App For That
Elephant Cock (Godless Exclusive Novelette)

www.splatploitation.com

Printed in Great Britain
by Amazon

25505525R00076